CARLA?

The truth was, I felt excited, nervous, and happy, all at the same time. I had tried to imagine what it would be like meeting Carla for the very first time, but my mind balked whenever I tried to picture her face. Would she be beautiful, with long, flowing hair, as Erin predicted? Or would she be cute or funny or athletic? Or would she be — I hated to think this — really stuck-up and unpleasant?

"There she is!" I said excitedly, as a beautiful girl with long black hair walked out of the airport gate. She was wearing a tiny miniskirt with stiletto heels, and I heard Michael give an appreciative whistle. "Cool it!" I hissed, nudging him in the ribs.

"Carla?" my mother asked expectantly. The girl stared at her as if she were crazy, and laughed.

"Marsha," she said.

My mother stared at me. "Well, she *looked* Italian," I said defensively.

"She looked fantastic," Michael said, obviously intrigued. "But where's Carla?"

"A good question," Mom muttered.

Look for these and other **Apple Paperbacks** in your local bookstores!

ALMOST LIKE A SISTER

M.L. Kennedy

AN
APPLE
PAPERBACK

SCHOLASTIC INC.
New York Toronto London Auckland Sydney

Scholastic Books are available at special discounts for quantity purchases for use as premiums, promotional items, retail sales through specialty market outlets, etc. For details contact: Special Sales Manager, Scholastic Inc., 730 Broadway, New York, NY 10003.

ISBN 0-590-33957-5

12 11 10 9 8 7 6 5 4 3 2 1   6 7 8 9/8 0 1/9

Printed in the U.S.A.   01

First Scholastic Printing, December 1986

ALMOST LIKE A SISTER

For Julie Fasciana

Chapter 1

It was three o'clock on a meltingly hot August afternoon, when I got what I'll always think of as "The Big News." My best friend, Erin Thompson, and I were sprawled on my bed, flipping through a *Seventeen* magazine, trying to figure out what the kids would be wearing to school in September.

As usual, we couldn't agree on anything. I voted for denim miniskirts and jelly shoes, while Erin insisted that cropped pants with Captain Kangaroo pockets would really be hot. We were arguing over a brown-and-white striped pantsuit with the sleeves rolled up when my mom walked in, grinning from ear to ear.

"What's up?" I said, feeling myself start to smile, too. From the dazed, happy look on her face, I was sure she'd just won the Publisher's Clearinghouse Sweepstakes.

She sat down very gingerly on the edge of my bed, as though she didn't trust her legs to hold her up. "Jamie," she said, a little breathlessly, "how would you like to have a sister?"

"Mom!" I yelled. "You don't mean you're — " I was so excited, I nearly tumbled to the floor.

"No," she laughed. "What I had in mind isn't quite that dramatic. Look, this is a last-minute kind of thing, but how would you feel about having an Italian teenager live with us for a semester? We have to make up our minds fast, because she's arriving in the United States next week to start her sophomore year of high school."

"You mean she's an exchange student?" Erin piped up. "Hey, that's neat! How did you find her?"

"I didn't," Mom said. "I ran into Mrs. Miller at the bank and she asked me if we'd like to be a host family in the International Exchange Program. The Millers had a German boy live with them last year, and it worked out very well. In fact, she's so enthusiastic about the program that she volunteered to find homes for this new batch of kids." She settled herself more comfortably on the bed, and tucked her long legs under her. "I told her I'd have to talk it over with you."

"How long would she be here?" I asked.

"Just till mid-December. She'll leave right before the Christmas holidays." She paused and looked at me very seriously. "I want you to think it over carefully, Jamie, because you'll be the one who'll be spending a lot of time with this girl."

"It would be almost like having a sister," I said thoughtfully.

"That's right," Mom agreed. "She'd share your room, and she'd go to Copley High with you every day."

"We could introduce her to all our friends, and show her the ropes, Mrs. Hogan." Erin smiled at me. "Does she speak English?" she asked suddenly.

"Yes, her English is supposed to be very good." Mom unfolded a computer printout and glanced at it. "We don't know too much about her, but her name is Carla Santini, and she's from Rome. And she's fourteen, just like you, Jamie." She paused. "She was on a waiting list for the foreign exchange program, and suddenly they had an opening for one more student."

"So she needs a place to stay," I said slowly.

"She needs more than that," Mom answered crisply. "She needs a family. If we're not prepared to make a real commitment to her, then we shouldn't invite her to stay with us. I think it would be a lot of fun having her here, but there may be some rough spots, too. After all, Carla will have some big adjustments to make — a new country, a new language. . . . She'll need a lot of help and encouragement every step of the way." For a moment, no one said anything. "Well, what do you think?"

I looked at Mom and smiled. "I think I better start cleaning my room."

"Fantastic!" Mom said excitedly. "I'll call Mrs. Miller right now, and then I'll talk to the principal and get Carla registered at Copley." Erin and I exchanged a look and smiled. My mom gets really hyper sometimes, and she was talking a mile a minute. "And I'd better check to see what time her flight's arriving at the airport."

Suddenly Mom stopped talking, and paused to think for a minute. "Maybe I'm crazy," she said. "Do you really think we can get everything done by next week?"

"Sure we can," I said encouragingly. "Just make out some of your famous lists, and Michael and I will divide up the work." Actually, I was being a little optimistic. Michael is my eighteen-year-old brother, and he's not wild about doing stuff around the house. The only way to get any work out of him at all is to write all his chores on a piece of paper and hand it to him.

"That's just what we need — some lists!" she exclaimed. "I'll do that right away."

She started to dart out the door, and stopped. She looked around my room, blinked in disbelief, and did one of her Jekyll-and-Hyde mood changes. "Jamie, this room is a disgrace — a complete disaster! Will you please clean it up immediately?"

She went out the door, then, just as Erin caught my eye and winked.

"Mothers," I said softly, and she laughed. I sat down on the edge of my desk, a little dazed, and wondered where to begin with my room.

"Carla Santini. I can just picture her," Erin said dreamily. She flopped on the bed and squinted her eyes tightly shut.

"You can?" I asked a little nervously.

"Uh-huh," she answered. "Can't you? Tall and beautiful, with long, dark hair, big emerald eyes, and a dynamite figure."

A dynamite figure. I immediately sucked in my stomach. For the first time, I stopped wondering what I would think of Carla. What would she think of *me*?

"Erin," I said abruptly. "If you were Carla, what would you need to make you happy here?"

Erin opened her eyes and giggled.

"That's easy. Boys," she said promptly. "Tall ones, short ones, smart ones."

"Be serious," I pleaded. "I mean, what can I do to make sure that Carla likes it here?" Suddenly the gravity of the situation hit me. I'd be sharing my room — and my life — with a total stranger for four whole months!

"Well, if you want an honest opinion," she said, looking slowly around my room.

"I do!" I scrambled to my feet.

"She'll need some closet space," Erin said practically. "After all, she's probably bringing a ton of clothes with her. From the looks of things, she'll have to stash them under the bed."

I followed Erin's gaze to my closet door, which was wedged open by three pairs of shoes. "I'll clean out my closet," I said desperately. "Help me decide what to save and what to throw out."

"Okay," Erin said, snapping to life. "But if I were you, I'd open a thrift shop."

"Very funny," I said.

We worked steadily on my closet for the next hour and had almost finished when it was time for Erin to go home for dinner. I had tried to be really fair about it, and had crunched all my clothes to one side so that Carla would have half the space.

"It's going to be tough for Carla," Erin

said as she was getting ready to leave. She ran a comb through her short black hair and got on her bike.

"Coming to a strange place, you mean?"

"*Everything*," she said feelingly. "Just think how *we* felt freshman year. We were in a brand-new school, and we felt totally out of it."

"At least we spoke the language," I offered. And we had each other, I thought silently. Erin and I have known each other since third grade, and we're such good friends, we can practically read each other's minds.

"And we had our families," Erin offered. She tucked her red tank top back in the waistband of her shorts, and clapped her Walkman earphones to her head. "But poor Carla," she said sympathetically. "She'll be all alone."

"We'll just have to show her that she's got friends," I said assuringly. "And that we'll really — " I stopped talking when I realized that Erin had already flipped up the volume on her Walkman and was mouthing the words to a hit song.

"See you tomorrow!" she said in an unnaturally loud voice, and I waved as she pedaled down the driveway.

Mom was talking on the phone when I

went back to the house, so I decided to take another look at my room, trying to see it from a stranger's eyes. Would Carla like it? Do Italian teenagers cover their walls with posters of rock stars? Practically every square inch of my blue-and-white striped wallpaper is plastered with giant blowups of Bruce Springsteen and Madonna. My dressing table is littered with souvenirs from dozens of concerts, and my record collection takes up two shelves of my bookcase. If Carla isn't a rock 'n roll fan, I'm in big trouble, I decided.

I was making a halfhearted effort to clean up my dresser top, when I suddenly caught a glimpse of myself in the mirror. Would I measure up to Carla's idea of "a typical American teenager"? I made a quick inventory: long, brown hair swept back in a ponytail; big, clear blue eyes that were definitely my best feature; and a smile that Erin calls my "Flipper grin." She says I look like a dolphin, because I always seem to be smiling, even when I don't mean to be. My mouth just turns up at the edges naturally. Sometimes it's a handicap, because no one ever believes me when I say I'm in a bad mood.

"Jamie!" My mother's voice jolted me back to the present. "Andy's on the phone, but don't talk long, because I've got calls to make!"

I turned too quickly to grab the receiver and banged my shin on my night table.

"Ooh . . . ow. . . . Hi!" I wailed.

My boyfriend, Andy Parker, chuckled and said tolerantly, "Is that a new greeting, or should I hang up and call again?"

"You could at least be a little sympathetic. I just about splintered my kneecap rushing to talk to you," I said coolly.

"That's the kind of devotion I like," he teased me. "I sure wish I didn't have to work tonight. I'd much rather be with you instead of ten pounds of pizza dough."

"There's always next Saturday night," I said softly. I felt a little warm glow inside and started to smile. Andy and I have been dating for over a year, and he's definitely one of the cutest boys at Copley. Erin thinks he's adorable, and is always telling me that a lot of girls would like to go out with him. He's got sandy hair, a great smile, and these amazing brown eyes with very long, dark lashes.

"I know," he sighed. "But I didn't want to wait a week to spend time with you."

"But what would Pappy's do without you?" I kidded him. "You know you've got a magic touch with pepperoni. Mr. Androtti always says so." Andy works every other Saturday night at Pappy's, a local pizza joint. Sometimes I go there with Erin to see him, but usually he's up to his elbows in flour and is much too busy to say more than a quick hello.

"Yeah," he said ruefully. "Well, I can think of better ways to spend the evening. What are you up to?"

"I'm cleaning my room," I started to say, and then stopped. I had been so glad to hear from him, I had forgotten all about Carla. "You're not going to believe this, Andy, but the most fantastic thing has happened. We're getting an exchange student!"

"Really? A he or a she?" If I didn't know better, I could have thought that Andy sounded a little worried.

"A girl, Andy. Her name's Carla Santini and she's from Rome. She's going to live with us for four months."

We talked about Carla for a few minutes, and then I looked up to see my mother doing an elaborate pantomime in the doorway. She was making a throat-slashing motion, like a director on a movie set.

I got the message. "I guess I've got to go now, Andy. My mother needs to use the phone."

"I've got to head down to Pappy's anyway," he said regretfully. "Mr. Androtti's got this new topping I'm supposed to push tonight — pineapple-sausage."

"Yucch!" I said sympathetically. "He should stick to pepperoni and cheese."

"I think so, too." There was a pause, and then Andy said softly, "Don't forget to miss me a little, okay?"

"You know I will," I told him. I hung up quickly, before my mother had a chance to go through another charade, and followed her out to the kitchen.

"It's smorgasbord time," Mom said gaily. She started pulling leftovers out of the refrigerator just as Michael and Dad came through the back door together. A couple of times a week, Mom decides that cooking is a giant waste of time, and that everyone should fend for themselves. She told me once that if she had spent as many hours studying as she did cooking, she could have become an expert on, say, the United Nations, or become fluent in Sanskrit.

Secretly, I'm inclined to agree with her, but it's hard to be idealistic when you're facing a scrawny baked chicken and a Tupperware dish of wobbly Jell-O. Mom had already told Dad and Michael the news about Carla, and we were all in a giddy state of shock when we sat down to dinner.

"Hey, Mom, are you going to try to cook Italian when Carla gets here next week?" Michael kidded her.

"I'm not going to run out and buy a pasta machine, if that's what you mean," she retorted. "The reason Carla's coming to the States is to absorb *American* culture." She picked over the remains of a chicken breast like an amateur archeologist.

"Yeah, but does she have to absorb leftovers, too?" Michael laughed at his own joke, and Mom rolled her eyes.

"Maybe *you'd* like to do the cooking," she said tartly, and for once Michael had nothing to say. He and Dad believe that cooking is a noble occupation, as long as they don't have to do it.

We talked about Carla during the rest of the meal, and I guess each of us was wondering what she'd be like. I knew Dad could hardly wait to talk to her about the Italian financial system. He's a stockbroker, and he can talk for hours about futures and commodities and investment bonds. Mom and I try to listen politely, but when he gets heavily into it, our eyes start to glaze over. I guess he figured Carla would be a new, more appreciative, audience.

Knowing Michael, he was probably wondering if Carla was cute. I almost told him what Erin said about green eyes and a dynamite figure, and then stopped. The last thing I needed was a lovesick Michael moping around the house and combing his hair a million times a day. Last summer he had this unbelievable crush on Sylvia Roberts, and had actually bleached his hair just because she'd said she liked guys who were blond. He had denied doing it, of course, but I saw the empty box of Frost and Tip under his bed.

Mom nibbled at her dessert, and seemed more preoccupied than ever. She had a hazy, faraway look in her eyes, so I figured she was either planning some new show at the art gallery where she works, or was making out her grocery list. I was wrong. When she caught me looking at her, she smiled and pointed to her watch.

"Do you know what? Next Saturday, at this exact moment, Carla will be sitting here with us." She patted an empty chair beside her, and the three of us looked dutifully at it. "It's hard to believe, isn't it?"

"It sure is," I said, panicky, thinking of my room, which was now a semi-disaster. "I hope this week crawls by. I've got a million things to do before she gets here."

Mom grinned and snapped her fingers. "If I were you, I'd get started," she said, "because I've got the feeling next Saturday is going to be here before you know it."

Chapter 2

Have you ever noticed that time seems to stand still when you're waiting for something to happen? The next few days dragged by like frames in a slow-motion movie, as Mom and I worked to get the house in shape for Carla's arrival. By Friday, my room was so clean it looked practically unlived-in, and the kitchen was stocked with enough soft drinks and snacks to feed my entire class at Copley High.

Suddenly it was Saturday, and I found myself in the backseat of our station wagon, heading toward Kennedy International Airport. We live in Westchester, which is just north of Manhattan. The weekend traffic was murder, as usual, but Dad had left in plenty of time, and we found ourselves with half an hour to kill at the terminal. I wandered around the gift shop, checking out the T-shirts and posters, and wishing the butterflies in my stomach would calm down.

"Feeling a little nervous?" I hadn't heard my mother come up behind me, and when she spoke, I jumped.

"Does that answer your question?" I said, and she laughed. The truth was, I felt excited, nervous, and happy, all at the same time. I had tried to imagine what it would be like meeting Carla for the very first time, but my mind balked whenever I tried to picture her face. Would she be beautiful, with long, flowing hair, as Erin predicted? Or would she be cute or funny or athletic? Or would she be — I hated to think this — really stuck-up and unpleasant?

I didn't have time to think about it anymore, because my father suddenly appeared at the door of the gift shop. "They just announced her flight," he said cheerfully, motioning toward the main gate. He and Michael had made this cardboard sign with THE HOGANS written on it in red magic marker. I felt kind of silly, standing there behind the sign like a human billboard, but Dad said that it was the only way Carla would be able to identify us. After all, we didn't know what she looked like, and she had no idea at all what to expect. All she knew was that she was meeting an American family with a couple of teenage kids.

"There she is!" I said excitedly, as a beautiful girl with long, black hair walked up to us. She was wearing a tiny miniskirt with stiletto heels, and I heard Michael give an appreciative whistle. "Cool it!" I hissed, nudging him in the ribs.

"Carla?" my mother asked expectantly. The girl stared at her as if she were crazy, and laughed.

"Marsha," she said.

My mother stared at me. "Well, she *looked* Italian," I said defensively.

"She looked fantastic," Michael said, obviously intrigued. "But where's Carla?"

"A good question," Mom muttered. She scanned the passengers who were rushing by us, and frowned. "You don't think she missed the flight, do you?"

"I think we would have heard." Dad tried to sound reassuring, but I could tell he was worried, too. There were hardly any teenagers arriving on Flight 705, and except for a handful of stragglers, the corridor was nearly empty. Where was she?

Then I noticed a dark-haired boy in a white suit strolling casually through the security check, and I did a double take. I guess he caught my eye because he was one of the best-looking boys I had ever seen in my life. But I could tell just from the way he moved, and the smug expression on his face, that he was really stuck on himself.

"I think we'll have to call Mrs. Miller," I heard Mom say, and then she gave a funny little gasp.

I turned around and could hardly believe what happened next. The boy in the white suit was kissing her hand! I nearly flipped, especially when I heard him say with this really beautiful accent, "Señora Hogan? I am Carlo Santini."

"*C-Carlo?*" Mom stammered. She looked as shocked as I felt, and she turned help-lessly to Dad.

"You are the Hogans, no?" the boy asked, still smiling at her, treating us all to a set of dazzling white teeth.

"No, I mean, yes," she said hastily. "We're the Hogans."

His grin grew even wider. "*Buono!* I am your exchange student."

I dimly remembered that *buono* meant good in Italian. Good? If *this* was our ex-change student, this was a disaster!

"Welcome to the United States, Carlo," Dad said, finding his voice at last. He stuck out his hand. "I'm Richard Hogan, this is my wife, Andrea, and our children, Michael and Jamie."

Michael managed to smile and shake hands with Carlo, but I was still in a state of shock, and Dad pushed me forward.

"Welcome . . . to the United States," I muttered, parroting Dad's greeting. My mouth was dry, and the words stuck in my throat. I drew my hand back as quickly as I could, and stared at Mom and Dad. Wasn't anyone going to say anything?

"What do you say we head down and get your luggage?" Dad finally managed in a normal voice, like there was nothing wrong. He tossed the car keys to Michael, who grabbed them eagerly. "Son, why don't you get the car, and we'll meet you out front."

"Sure, Dad." Michael grinned at me, like he was really getting a kick out of the whole thing, and disappeared through the glass doors. He actually seemed pleased that Carlo was a boy. The next thing you know, he'll be asking him if he plays soccer, I thought disgustedly.

I had never felt at such a loss in my whole life. My carefully rehearsed speech to "Carla" fell apart, and I couldn't think of a thing to say.

Except what was on my mind. We were waiting for Carlo's luggage to appear, when I couldn't stand it any longer.

"You were supposed to be a girl!" I blurted out.

Carlo looked puzzled and gave a very carefree shrug. "A girl?" he said slowly. He laughed, then. "As you can see, I am a boy." He smiled at my parents, like it was all some wonderful joke, and waited for me to join in.

I glared at him. "On the application form," I said icily. I fished in my pocketbook for the computer printout and practically threw it at him. "Look, it says you're a girl. Carla Santini. *Not* Carlo."

"Oh yes," he said, and flashed that slow, infuriating smile. "I noticed that."

"You *noticed* it?" I yelled. "Why didn't you say something? Why didn't you correct it?"

Carlo's smile faded a little, as though he was getting bored with the whole conversation. "Well, in your country, everything is these computers nowadays. And they make many mistakes, no? In Italy, it is different. I do not understand computers. I am not a technical person."

"Not a technical person! All you had to do was pick up the phone and tell somebody that they made a mistake." I glared at him, waiting for him to try to defend himself. When he shrugged again, I really got mad. "You misled everyone," I said furiously. Mom shot me a warning look.

"Misled?" He formed the word carefully, like he wasn't really sure what it meant. "My vocabulary . . ." he began apologetically.

My mother decided to get in the act. "Don't worry about it, Carlo. You didn't mislead anyone," she said, glaring at me. "It's just a little misunderstanding, that's all. The important thing is that you're here, and we're very happy to have you." She gave him a warm smile and his face lit up. It was obvious the two of them were going to get along terrifically.

"You must forgive me, Jamie," he said, with a dramatic sigh. "I am not one for the paperwork. I never bother with ... forms." He gave a little wave toward the piece of paper in my hand. "I did not think it really mattered."

"No, of course you didn't," I said through gritted teeth. My first impression of Carlo Santini was correct. He was the most conceited jerk I had ever met!

I stared silently out the car window all the way back home, ignoring puzzled looks from my parents and Michael. If Carlo realized that I was completely disgusted with him, he didn't let on. He acted like he was having the time of his life, smiling and laughing, entertaining my parents with funny stories about his relatives. Apparently, Carlo came from a well-to-do family, and had lived all over the world. This, however, was his first trip to the U.S.

"Ah, this is my dream," he said happily, looking out the window. "Ever since I was a little boy, I have wanted to come to the States." I was hoping Carlo would ignore me, when suddenly I could feel his eyes on me.

"Jamie," he began in a friendly voice, "I guess I will be going to your high school, no? We are the same age, I believe."

"That's right," I said as coolly as I could. Carlo looked at me expectantly, obviously waiting for me to say something else, but I kept my eyes glued on the scenery.

"Hey, you'll really like Copley High, man." Michael jumped in to fill in the gap. "They've got a terrific football team, and some great computer courses, and the girls — wow!"

The two of them laughed, and I felt like kicking Michael. They were actually getting to be friends! It was bad enough to be tricked into getting Carlo, but now I was being betrayed by my own brother!

"Are you interested in sports?" I heard Michael ask Carlo.

"Oh yes, I play several," Carlo said easily. "But my favorite is soccer."

"Somehow I knew it would be," I muttered.

"One of the most exciting moments in my life was when I got to meet the great

Pelé after a match," Carlo continued.

"You met Pelé!" Michael's eyes were practically popping out of his head, and it was a miracle he didn't fall off the seat.

"At a reception in Brazil," Carlo said in an elaborately casual voice.

"He's fantastic," Michael said softly. "I'd give anything to meet him."

"Well, maybe if you visit me in my country, we can arrange it. My uncle is very friendly with him."

"That would be great, just great," Michael said, almost delirious with joy.

I was so disgusted, I didn't say one single word for the rest of the trip. The really annoying part was that everyone else was having such a good time, they didn't even notice. I decided that there were two possibilities: Either Michael and my parents were terrific actors, or they were really thrilled with our "guest." As far as I was concerned, I would have liked to see Carlo hop on the next plane back to Rome. It's too bad exchange students can't be recalled, like defective cars, I thought idly.

The phone was ringing as soon as we walked in the kitchen, and I snatched the receiver off the hook.

"What's she like?" Erin's voice, warm and excited, raced over the wires.

"Uh, hang on while I take this in my room, will you?" I turned to Mom. "Would you hang this up for me?" I said very sweetly.

She gave me a puzzled look, but I marched into the bedroom and firmly shut the door. My room looked bare, and for a minute, I missed the familiar clutter. All for Carlo, I thought angrily. All for nothing.

"Well, tell me all about her," Erin was saying impatiently. "Is she beautiful, is she nice — "

"No!" I barked angrily. "She's not beautiful, and she's not nice. What's more, she isn't even a she. She's a *he!*"

"What?" Erin croaked.

"She's a *he*," I repeated furiously.

"But that's impossible," Erin said weakly.

Carlo's infectious laugh drifted in from the kitchen and I winced. "Hah! Tell that to Carlo."

"Carlo?"

"That's right. Carlo Santini," I added, anticipating her next question. "There was some mix-up with the computer printout. An *o* got changed to an *a* and that's how we got Carlo. We're stuck with this Italian guy, instead of a girl."

"Hmmm," Erin said thoughtfully. "An

Italian *guy*. Are you sure there aren't some possibilities there?"

"What do you mean?" I snapped.

"Well, you know," she giggled. "Italian boys are supposed to be very romantic."

"Romantic! He's obnoxious." I crunched a pillow behind my head and gave a big sigh. "The next four months are going to be the worst in my whole life."

"Maybe not," Erin said mischievously. "I think he sounds sort of interesting."

"What makes you say that?" I asked coldly. "You don't even know anything about him."

"So tell me," Erin said innocently. "What does he look like?"

I tried to be objective. "He's okay-looking," I said after a moment.

"Just okay-looking?"

"He's about five-ten and has black hair and dark eyes. He's got a square jaw, and very good teeth — " Erin was already bursting with excitement.

"I want to meet him," she said suddenly.

"What?"

"I want to meet him. You're not eating dinner yet, are you?"

"No, but — "

"I'll be right over."

She hung up before I could say another word. This just wasn't my day.

Chapter 3

"I can only stay a minute," Erin was saying to my mother half an hour later. Mom was cutting hefty slices of the double fudge cake I had made to welcome our guest. I had carefully dribbled *Buon giorno, Carla* on it in white frosting, and Michael joked that I was off by one letter. I was the only one who didn't laugh.

"We'll just have to make that *a* into an *o*," Dad said heartily, and everyone grinned at Carlo, who sat there smiling like the Cheshire cat. I tried to crack a smile, but it felt like my face would crack instead. What was there to joke about? Didn't anybody else realize that we were in the middle of a major disaster? I could hardly wait to get Erin alone in my room, and tell her what a creep Carlo was.

"Well, at least stay for some cake," Mom urged. Erin didn't need any coaxing. She immediately sat down at the kitchen table next to Carlo. Only stay a minute? It was obvious that wild horses couldn't drag her away!

"Hey, Jamie, I'm glad you cook better than you spell," Michael said, in what had to be the dumbest remark of the year. Naturally, that sent everyone into gales of laughter all over again. Michael just looked pleased.

Carlo smiled tolerantly and shook his head. "It's only off by one letter, and anyway, how could you have known? It was very nice of you to make this for me, Jamie."

Everybody picked up their forks then, or I should say, everybody but Erin. She was staring at Carlo, smiling idiotically. She had had the same kind of look on her face when we went to a Bruce Springsteen concert last year, and I felt like kicking her under the table. If I didn't know her better, I would have said she *liked* Carlo, but of course that was impossible. I took a giant bite of fudge cake, and wondered when we could politely excuse ourselves. I could hardly wait to get Erin alone.

"I've always been interested in Italian culture," Erin was saying in this sappy voice. She was leaning forward, practically nose to nose with Carlo, and I thought I saw her flutter her eyelashes.

"Really?" Carlo said with a lazy smile. "Have you visited my country?"

"Not exactly," she hedged.

Not exactly? The closest Erin has come to Italy is a Double-Pepperoni Delight at Pappy's Pizza.

"But it's always been a dream of mine to go to Florence," she told him.

"Ah, *Firènze*," he said, giving the famous city its Italian name. "When you come to Italy, I will show you around," he said grandly. "*Roma, Firènze, Napoli.* . . . I will show you all the sights."

"That would be fantastic," she said breathlessly. "Maybe we could go next summer, Jamie. And in the meantime, Carlo could teach us Italian. I've always been fascinated by foreign languages."

I almost reminded her she got a C-minus in French last year, but restrained myself. After all, even though she had rotten taste in guys, she was still my best friend. "He's here to learn *English*," I said curtly, but she didn't get the hint.

"Oh, yes, I know that," she said, flushing a little. "I just meant. . . ." Her voice trailed off unhappily, and Carlo reached over and squeezed her hand.

"No problem, Erin. We will have — how do you call it? A trade-out," he said reassuringly. "I will teach all of you Italian, and you will teach me English." He smiled, like he had just solved all the world's problems.

"You'll have your hands full with English, man," Michael said. "Not that your English isn't great," he said hastily, "but there's lots of slang you'll have to learn."

"Ah, I have a book with me. Just a minute, I get it." He stood up, murmuring "*Scusa*," to my mother, and disappeared in the direction of the hall. Everyone was quiet for a minute while we heard him rummaging in his suitcase.

"Nice kid," Dad said to no one in particular.

"He certainly is polite," my mother said in a low voice. She leaned back in her chair, and I noticed that she looked a little tired. "Well, this has really been a day full of surprises," she added, looking around the table. Her eyes rested on me and she looked like she was going to say something, but just then, Carlo returned, holding up a battered paperback of American slang.

"My father gave me this," he said proudly, sitting next to Erin. "Look inside." He flipped it open to the first page, and Erin stared at it blankly.

"Ah, *stupido*," he said apologetically, lightly slapping his forehead with his palm.

"I forget it is written in Italian. I read it for you." He paused like an actor, to make sure he had our complete attention. " 'To my son, Carlo. I hope you enjoy the United States of America as much as I did. Papa.' "

To my surprise, Carlo's eyes looked suspiciously wet. Was he homesick already?

"When was your father over here?" Mom said quickly.

Carlo brushed his hand rapidly over his eyes before answering. "It was in the fifties, I think."

"Is that when he bought the book?" Erin asked incredulously. When Carlo nodded, she smothered a laugh, and said gently, "I'm afraid it won't be much help to you. Carlo. It's way out-of-date."

"Oh, no, I don't think so," Carlo said seriously. "My father said there are many favorite American expressions in here. For example, you are really a gorgeous doll, Erin, and Michael here, is a cool cat."

There was a moment of uncomfortable silence, as Carlo waited for us to say something.

"That is correct, no?" he said, his movie-star features starting to crumble into a frown.

"Carlo . . ." I began, but Mom stopped me with a look.

"I don't think we need to work on Carlo's English the first day he's here, do we, honey?" Her voice was overly bright as she stood up to clear the table. "I think it's much more important that we help him relax and feel at home. Jamie," she said with a brittle smile, "why don't you and Michael show Carlo his room?"

"I'm not sure . . ." I started blankly. I looked helplessly at Michael, who scraped his chair back noisily.

"I hope you don't mind bunk beds, Carlo," he said in a friendly way. "I usually sleep on the bottom one, but if you don't like heights, we can switch."

"Bunk beds? What is that?" Carlo looked puzzled.

"C'mon, I'll show you. And bring that book along," Michael said firmly. "You've got some catching up to do."

"I think he's really neat," Erin said a little later. We had finally escaped to the privacy of my room, and I had treated Erin to a full account of Carlo's failings. Oddly enough, she seemed totally unimpressed by what I had to say. In fact, I was surprised to see that she was going out of her way to defend him.

"Erin," I said, as patiently as I could, "he's rude, conceited, and obnoxious." I paused, trying to think of one really insulting word to describe him. "And he's probably a chauvinist pig."

"A chauvinist pig?"

I knew that would get her. "I'm almost sure of it," I said seriously. "Did you notice that he didn't even carry his plate to the sink? He just trotted after Michael like he expected Mom to clean up after him."

"I'm not sure that qualifies him as a chauvinist pig," Erin said with a smile. "Are you positive you're not just looking for something to dislike about him?"

"Looking for something!" I said indignantly. "That's a laugh. I don't *have* to look for things. I practically trip over them!"

"Well, I think he seems really nice," she repeated in this calm, infuriating way. "I'd really love it if I had him as a brother for a few months." She had a dreamy look in her eyes.

I took a good look at Erin and I realized something else. She was wearing her best linen pants — the ones that melt into a million wrinkles if you even breathe on them — and three shades of eyeshadow. Her nails were painted a frosty pink, and her black hair was shining. Why was she decked out like the reigning Miss America, just to come over to my house on a Saturday afternoon? It looked very suspicious.

"Trying out for the Miss Makeup award?" I asked unkindly, and was pleased when I saw her flinch.

"I, uh, was just experimenting with some eyeshadow before I called you," she said, biting her lip.

"Sure," I said briefly, not believing a word.

She glanced at her watch and made a face. "Hey, I didn't realize it was so late. Mom will shoot me — I was supposed to make dinner." She checked herself in the mirror and said hesitantly, "Will you say good-bye to Carlo for me?"

I rolled my eyes in disbelief, and she flushed. "Look Jamie, just because you think he's a jerk . . ." she began.

"I'll say good-bye for you," I said flatly, as she picked up her red shoulder bag and headed for the kitchen. I didn't bother walking her out to the driveway the way I usually did, and she looked a little hurt.

It was amazing. Carlo had only been with us for a few hours, and he had already put me at odds with my best friend. It was going to be a long four months.

We had a late dinner, and I was happy when Mom came down to the family room around ten and suggested that everyone turn in early.

"I know you guys are enjoying yourselves," she said, trying not to yawn, "but it's been a long day." Michael griped a little, because he was right in the middle of a pool game with Dad, but I noticed that Carlo flashed Mom a grateful look. He had dark circles under his eyes, and his olive skin looked suddenly pale.

I zipped into the shower to avoid a tense good-night scene, and stood under the pounding water for a long time. By the time I got out, the house was quiet, but I could see a light on under Michael's door. I listened carefully, and heard a soft murmur of voices followed by a burst of masculine laughter. Michael's found a friend, I thought resentfully.

So Michael was happy, Mom and Dad were happy, and Carlo seemed ecstatic at his new home. The only person left out of this fantastic arrangement was yours truly.

When I woke up the next morning, bright sunlight was streaming across my bedspread, and a warm breeze puffed out the muslin curtains at the window.

I rolled over on my stomach, glanced at the clock, and stretched luxuriously. What a terrific day, I thought. The perfect day for going to the beach with Andy, or taking a picnic to the park with Erin, or maybe just taking a long bike ride out to —

Then it hit me. Carlo! How could I have forgotten? I flopped over on my back, my good mood shattered. Right this moment, that obnoxious Italian pest was sleeping just a few yards away. And he was going to be here for the next four months. An eternity.

It was eight o'clock on a Sunday morning, I reminded myself. With any luck at all, Carlo wouldn't be getting up for hours. I could grab a quick breakfast, and then zip out somewhere. With that pleasant thought in mind, I staggered into the kitchen with a shiny face and tousled hair, clutching my tattered robe around me.

But when I got to the kitchen, I reeled backward in surprise. Carlo was sitting at the kitchen table, wearing a bright yellow shirt and carefully pressed white pants. He raised his cup in greeting, like an actor in a coffee commercial.

"Buon giorno! Good morning," he said, and flashed a winning smile. He jumped out of his seat, whether to embrace me, or pull out my chair, I didn't know. I wasn't taking any chances, though, so I plopped myself in one of the blue canvas director's chairs before he could reach me.

"Good morning," I muttered. I'm not a

morning person, even under the best of circumstances, and Carlo's smiling face didn't exactly brighten my mood. Plus — and I hate to admit this — it was embarrassing to have Carlo see me at my worst. I'm not one of these people who jumps out of bed looking terrific. My hair always looks like it died sometime during the night, and my skin has a sickly pallor. Whenever I go to slumber parties, my friends' mothers always take one look at me at the breakfast table, and ask me if I'm sick!

I could feel Carlo's eyes on me, and I had a wild impulse to run back and get some blusher. I stared back defiantly, determined to tough it out.

"How about some coffee?" he offered. "It is not espresso, but it's all I could find."

"I don't drink coffee," I told him, and then stopped in surprise. Carlo had found an elaborate silver coffee pot that Mom only drags out for parties, and had brewed a whole pot of murky brown liquid.

"I could not find the coffee beans," he said apologetically, "so I used what you call the quick coffee. It is strange, no?"

He pointed to a jar on the counter, and I tried not to smile. "Carlo, we call it *instant* coffee and it's not strange. We always use it. My mother wouldn't know a coffee bean if she fell over one."

"Really?" He seemed shocked at this news. "In Italy, we have the fresh-brewed coffee every morning at my house. Very strong, very good."

"Who makes the fresh-brewed coffee?" I asked him, putting on the kettle for a cup of tea.

"Ah, the housekeeper," he answered, waving a hand casually. "She is usually up first." He paused and bit into a piece of toast. "Also the *pane cioccolato*, the chocolate rolls."

"Also made by the housekeeper," I said wryly.

"But of course," he said, giving me a puzzled look.

"You're going to find life in *this* house very different," I started to say, just as Mom came in the kitchen.

"Well, are you two early birds planning your day?" she said cheerfully.

I could have killed her.

"No, we were just discussing coffee, actually." I was still standing at the stove, waiting for the water to boil.

"It's a nice day for the beach," she said, opening the kitchen window. "Or maybe a picnic."

"Uh-huh," I said, carefully noncommittal. She had practically read my mind, something she is very good at doing.

"Or horseback riding, or canoeing down at Palmer's Lake," she suggested.

She was beginning to sound like a social director.

She looked doubtfully at Carlo. "Unless you're tired from your trip, Carlo."

"Oh, no," he said, beaming. "I've had three cups of your quick coffee —"

"*Instant* coffee," I said under my breath.

"And now I'm ready to — how do you say it? Take on the world!" He was grinning from ear to ear and spread his arms wide in a theatrical gesture.

Mom laughed delightedly. "That's wonderful," she said, clapping her hands together. "Isn't that wonderful, Jamie?"

I yanked the whistling kettle off the stove so quickly, some of the boiling water sloshed out and burned my thumb.

"Wonderful," I agreed through clenched teeth. "Just wonderful."

Chapter 4

Carlo spent the next few days "settling in" with us, and it was obvious that nothing short of an earthquake would dislodge him from the Hogan family. He was an instant hit with everybody, and Mom just took it for granted that I would include him in all my plans.

"Isn't it nice that you have some time left before school starts?" she said cheerfully. "This way, you'll have a chance to introduce Carlo to all your friends." The trouble was, I didn't *want* to introduce Carlo to my friends, but there was no way to get out of it.

A few mornings later, I was lingering over my Orange Delight tea, wondering how I could unload Carlo for the day, when the kitchen phone rang.

"Jamie? I've got the most fantastic idea. Why don't we round up some of the kids and take Carlo to Palmer's Lake? We could pack a lunch and rent some rowboats. . . ."

I let Erin ramble on, while I slowly crumbled a piece of toast. I could feel Carlo's dark eyes on me, and I turned, embarrassed, and pretended to stare out the window.

"Well, that sounds great," I said, forcing a note of enthusiasm into my voice. "I'll have to check with Andy, of course. We were supposed to spend the day together."

She babbled on deliriously. "Perfect! I knew you'd like the idea. My mom says I can fry some chicken, and we can buy some potato salad on the way. Do you think you could bring the rest of the stuff — like some soda and chips and napkins? Oh, and something for dessert. Why don't you make some brownies? They're easy."

"Sure," I said tightly. It was bad enough to be suckered into spending the day with Carlo. Now I was baking brownies for him!

Carlo looked at me inquisitively when I hung up. "We're going out for the day?" he asked hopefully.

"That's right," I said, wishing I could think of a last-minute excuse to cancel. "Erin — you met her last Saturday — thought you might like to go to the lake with a bunch of kids." I crossed my fingers, and hoped he'd say no.

No such luck.

"*Buono!*" he said, breaking into that smile again. "That's swell."

I winced. Someday I'd have to get up my nerve to tell him about that fifties slang. At the moment, I had other worries.

"Let me check with my mom, and then I need to call Andy. He's my boyfriend," I explained.

"Oh, by all means, check with your boyfriend," Carlo said, with a twinkle in his eye. I was sure he was teasing me. He shrugged. "Who knows? He might object."

"I'm not asking his permission," I said hotly. "I'm calling him up to invite him to go with us."

"Ah." He gave me a tolerant smile, as I pushed my chair back and left the kitchen. When I got to my room, I closed the door and flopped on my bed the way I always do when I call Andy. I was still seething as I dialed Andy's number.

As if I needed Andy's permission to go to the lake! I thought angrily.

Unfortunately, I struck out with Andy. "You have to work today?" I wailed. "But you worked at Pappy's last night!"

"I know, but Mr. Androtti is running another special," Andy said patiently. "That pineapple number didn't go over too well, so he's trying something else. He needs the extra kitchen help today."

"But why?" I questioned, refusing to be convinced.

"Because we're going to work on a secret formula for a new topping. Something that will make Pappy's the number one pizza spot in town."

"What is it?" I asked sullenly. I hated the whiny note in my voice, but I couldn't help it. How could Andy let me down? Now I'd be spending the whole day with Carlo!

"I can't tell you," Andy said breezily. "I'm sworn to secrecy."

"You can't tell me?" I could hear my voice rising about eight octaves. "I don't believe this! Are you saying you don't trust me?"

"I told you, it's a secret." He sounded rushed, and a little annoyed. "And look, Jamie, I've really got to go. Dad wants me to mow the lawn before I leave for work."

I hung up, my spirits somewhere down around my ankles.

I was digging in my drawer for my bathing suit when the phone rang.

It was Andy. "Jamie? Why don't you stop by Pappy's around six with the gang? I take my break then. At least we'll have a few minutes together."

"Great!" I was so pleased, I forgot I was supposed to be annoyed with him. The day was shaping up. All I had to do was get through the next eight hours.

"I've always been fascinated by Roman emperors," Sherry Mitchell was saying in a syrupy voice. "I've always, like, admired them, you know?"

Carlo stretched lazily and reached for another hot dog. It was turning into a scorcher of a day, and the beach area of Palmer's Lake was already jammed with kids. He stared at Sherry, taking in her chamois bikini. It was held together by thin strips of leather and plastic beads, and I had to grudgingly admit that she looked fantastic.

"Really? Which ones?" he managed in a voice that was practically a yawn. Sherry had been knocking herself out for the past hour trying to get his attention, but I could tell she was wasting her time. She was lying on a narrow band of the beach blanket, smiling, giggling, trying to get as close to him as humanly possible. She'd talked nonstop from the moment she sat down, but Carlo had paid about as much attention to her as he did to the flies that buzzed annoyingly around us.

"Well, uh, all of them," she stammered, caught off guard.

Carlo gave a short laugh, and gazed out

at the lake. "Even Nero? Or maybe you prefer Caligula?"

"Cali — who?"

"Caligula," he repeated slowly. When Sherry flushed and looked puzzled, Carlo turned to me.

"Americans don't know much about European history, do they?" he said sadly. When I didn't answer, he stood up, drawing some admiring looks in his black bathing trunks and white T-shirt. He peeled off the T-shirt and announced abruptly, "I'm going in for a swim."

"Okay," I said flatly, not sure whether or not he wanted me to join him. "I'll save you some brownies."

He smiled then, and strode down toward the lake.

"Wow," Sherry breathed, the moment he was out of earshot. "He's gorgeous." She turned to Erin and said longingly, "How'd you like to have him as a houseguest for four months?"

"I'd die," Erin said simply. "Jamie doesn't know how lucky she is," she added, shooting me a reproachful look. "I wonder if he liked the food," she said after a moment. "He didn't eat much, did he?"

Who cares? I thought to myself. Things had gotten off to a bad start at lunch time. I had unpacked the plastic container of potato salad from Sutton's Deli, and Carlo had looked at it suspiciously.

"What is this?" He had poked a piece of potato with his fork as if it were going to bite him.

"It's potato salad," I had said patiently. "Very American."

"I know that. We have potato salad in my country," he had answered coolly, "but not like this. This is just potatoes . . . and . . . what is this white stuff?"

"Mayonnaise," Sherry had said helpfully.

"Mayonnaise. But where are the caraway seeds, the freshly ground mustard, the baby onions, the — what do you call them? The scallions."

"Carlo," I had said, trying to keep my voice even, "this is a picnic, not a gourmet restaurant. When you buy potato salad from a take-out place, this is what you get. It's *supposed* to look like that." I had put a big dollop of potato salad on his plate and had started serving the hot dogs.

The lifeguard's whistle made me jump, and I pulled my mind back to the present. I watched Carlo swimming gracefully in the lake for a few minutes and turned in time to hear Jeff Monroe say cuttingly, "Where are the baby onions?"

Jeff is a tall boy with blond hair, and

he and Erin have been dating for as long as I can remember. I suppose he was feeling a little jealous of Carlo by this time, and I can't say that I blame him.

Kurt Bailey, Sherry's date, hooted with laughter. "And where is — how do you call it? The freshly ground mustard!" he added, imitating Carlo's musical accent.

"Hey, you guys," I said halfheartedly. "Knock it off. He's a guest, you know?"

"I know," Jeff said flatly. "And as far as I'm concerned, he's outstayed his welcome."

"What are you talking about?" Erin objected. "He just got here. He's going to stay with the Hogans until Christmas."

"Don't remind me." Kurt put his head in his hands and gave a loud groan. "I think we should take up a collection to send him back to Italy." He laughed, but I knew he wasn't kidding.

"Very funny," Sherry said sharply. Kurt was gearing up for another insult, when she gave him a hard nudge in the ribs. "How would you like to be in a strange country, and not know anybody, and have to speak a strange language? Why don't you guys give him a break?"

"Yeah, come to think of it, English is pretty strange the way Carlo speaks it!" Jeff smiled, pleased with himself, but Erin didn't look amused.

"And what do you mean, give him a break? Why doesn't he give *us* a break?" Kurt said indignantly. "He hasn't even tried to be friends. He acts like we're a bunch of idiots."

"No he doesn't!" Erin insisted. "It's just that we're probably a lot different from the kids he knows back home. We're not what he's used to."

"Hey, that works two ways," Kurt said, hitching up the waistband on his brightly colored trunks. "He seems pretty weird to us."

Jeff grinned and was going to say something when he caught Erin glaring at him. He laughed, and stood up. "We're getting kind of low on soda. Why don't I go back to town and pick up some more? Anybody want to come along?"

"I'll come with you," Kurt said, scrambling to his feet. "We can let the girls work on their suntans." He dropped a piece of ice on Sherry's back, and she laughed and smacked his foot.

"The guys are impossible," Erin said, after they'd left.

"Jealousy," Sherry said simply. She tossed her long auburn hair over her shoulder and fastened it with a tortoiseshell barrette. "I hope Carlo doesn't pay any attention to them. I wouldn't want him to think that the guys don't like him. It's going to take some time," she said vaguely. "Just give them a couple of weeks, and they'll be great friends."

"I'm not too sure about that," I said, wondering what Andy's reaction to Carlo would be. "The problem isn't that he's foreign, the problem is he's so —"

"Cute," Erin interrupted mischievously.

"That's not what I was going to say," I retorted.

"No?" she asked innocently. She cupped her chin in her hand and pretended to stare at the lake, deep in thought. "I know!" she said suddenly. "If you don't like cute, how about adorable, handsome, gorgeous —"

"Don't forget sensational and fantastic," Sherry murmured, and then dissolved into laughter. "As far as I'm concerned, Carlo is just about the most perfect boy I've ever seen," she said a moment later, wiping her eyes. "There's nobody in the world who wouldn't think so, isn't that right, Erin?"

Erin looked at me and hesitated. Then she broke into a big grin. "Nobody in the world," she repeated.

They were both wrong. There was one person in the world, and it was my boyfriend, Andy Parker.

I got off on the wrong foot by being fifteen minutes late for our meeting at Pappy's, and Andy is a real stickler for promptness.

"I said *six*, not six-*fifteen*," he said irritably when he caught my eye over the counter that evening.

"I'm sorry," I said quickly. "But there was so much traffic."

"Then you should have left earlier," he said flatly. He was up to his elbows in pizza dough, and obviously not in the world's best mood.

"Well, I'm here now," I said brightly. I glanced at the back booth where the kids were sitting with Carlo. "Can't you come back and sit with us for a few minutes? There's someone I want you to meet."

A waitress bumped me with her elbow and waved a pile of orders at Andy. "Hey, Andy, hurry up with the double-anchovies. In another minute, those guys are gonna eat the tablecloth."

She glared at me, and I smiled politely.

"The place looks busier than ever," I said. "I guess you won't be taking a break."

"Business just picked up in the last fifteen minutes," Andy said curtly. "If you had been here on time, I could have taken my break with you."

I felt a soft touch on my elbow and whirled to face a smiling Carlo. "So this is your friend," he said politely, staring at Andy. He reached over the counter to shake hands with Andy, a big smile lighting up his expressive features.

Andy wiped his floury hands on his pants and looked at him suspiciously. "Hi," he said briefly. "You must be Carlo."

"Carlo Santini," Carlo answered, rolling out the syllables majestically.

"Yeah, well, it's really nice to meet you, Carlo, but as you can see, I'm up to my ears right now."

"Up to your ears?" Carlo looked bewildered.

"It's just an expression," I said quickly. "Andy is working on a new formula for pizza," I blurted out. I don't know what possessed me to say that, except that I felt kind of silly standing there with the guys eyeing each other.

"A new formula?" Carlo smiled. "But pizza has already been invented. It's been around for thousands of years."

"It has?" I asked in surprise. I had no way of knowing whether or not this was true, but Carlo had such a confident way of saying things, that people tended to believe him. Even me.

"Tell that to my boss," Andy sighed, digging into a new batch of sticky dough.

"He tried a pineapple topping that didn't

go over, so now he's looking for something new," I explained.

"Pineapple on pizza?" Carlo looked genuinely shocked.

"Hey, Andy! I need four more double-cheese and one large garbage. On the double!" the waitress called loudly. She turned to glare at me again, saw Carlo, and immediately smiled. Carlo smiled back, as if this happened to him all the time.

We joined the rest of the kids in the booth then, since it was obvious that Andy didn't have time to talk to us. When we had ordered cherry Cokes, Carlo turned to me, puzzled.

"Why would anyone order garbage?"

There was a long moment when no one said anything. "Garbage?" I repeated.

"Yes. The waitress said she needed a large garbage."

"Oh, *that*," I said, understanding at last. I started to laugh. "A garbage pizza isn't what you think it is. It's . . . it's a pizza with everything on it," I said finally. "You know, cheese, pepperoni, anchovies, mushrooms."

"Now I understand," he said, comprehending. "But you call it a garbage pizza?" he asked, shaking his head sadly, disapprovingly. "And they told me English was a logical language!"

Chapter 5

It was almost eight when we got home from Pappy's, and Mom was serving cold chicken and salads in the kitchen.

"We're just having a light supper tonight," she explained to Carlo. "I figured you and Jamie probably ate a lot of junk today at the beach."

"Oh yes," he said seriously. "A lot of junk. And we almost ate garbage at Pappy's. Many people did. It's very popular."

She raised her eyebrows questioningly, and I smiled. "I'll tell you about it later," I told her, sinking wearily into a chair. The sun and swimming had left me feeling drowsy, and I could hardly wait to eat and fall into bed.

We had just started dinner when Michael came rushing in from playing basketball. He greeted Carlo like they were long-lost friends. "Hey man! How're you doing?" he said, clapping Carlo enthusiastically on the back. "What did you think of Jamie's friends? The pits, right?"

Carlo looked helplessly at me. "The pits?"

"He means they're awful. Rock bottom," I explained, and speared a tomato.

"Oh, no," Carlo said generously. "They're nice, very nice. And I met the young man she steps out with."

Michael laughed so hard, I thought he would never be able to stop. "Steps out with?" he continued finally. "Where did you hear that?"

"Really, Michael," my mother murmured reproachfully. "People used to say that once, you know." She looked like she was having a hard time keeping a straight face.

"Carlo, believe me, *nobody* says 'steps out with.' " Michael grinned and piled his plate with sliced chicken and lots of salad.

"Well, what do you say when you are keeping company with someone?" Carlo persisted.

"No, you don't say keeping company, either," Michael said flatly. "You just say that so-and-so is your girl, or your main — I'll explain it all to you after dinner, okay? The first thing you have to do is forget everything in that slang book."

"Okay, Michael. That's hunky-dory."

Hunky-dory? Mom and Dad exchanged a look. Carlo didn't notice them, though, because he was busily digging into a salad like a starving man.

"So how was the lake?" Mom asked brightly.

"Okay," I answered, just as Carlo said, "Fun."

Fun? He certainly hadn't acted like he had enjoyed himself. Just the opposite, in fact. It was obvious that he had been bored out of his mind. Carlo and I looked at each other for a moment, when Mom piped up, "It's too bad you didn't get a chance to meet Andy. He's such a nice boy."

"Oh, we did meet him, Mom, when we were at Pappy's," I told her.

"That's nice," she said. "I hope the three of you can spend a lot of time together."

The three of us! I nearly choked on my macaroni salad. If Mom thought I was going to have an Italian chaperone trailing around after me on my dates, she was crazy!

Mom, Dad, and Carlo started talking about Italy then, and I raced through dinner, eager to escape to my room. I skipped dessert, even though it was lemon meringue pie, and at nine o'clock, I was lying in bed, happily talking to Erin on the phone.

"You don't know how glad I am that today's over," I said with relief. "I don't think I could have stood Carlo for five more minutes."

"I think he was wonderful!" Erin cried. "Sherry just called me and said she wants to triple again soon."

"Triple! Erin, are you out of your mind? Carlo's not my date. He's my . . . houseguest."

"Then I wish I could trade houses with you," Erin sighed.

"Hah! You wouldn't say that if you really knew him," I cautioned.

"Well, give me a chance to get to know him better," she said. "Why don't we have a party for him sometime? We could have it over here, and dance in the basement."

"Dance in the basement! Erin, will you get it through your head once and for all that he's not my date." Dance with Carlo? The mere thought of dancing with him made me gag. It would be like dancing with Michael!

"Well, please think about it," she pleaded. "You could bring Andy, and besides, your mother would really like to see us be nice to Carlo, wouldn't she?"

"I suppose so," I said slowly. "It's not such a bad idea, Erin. But don't plan on it yet. Let's just take it slow, okay?"

"Okay." There was a pause while she munched on something. "What are you going to wear to school tomorrow?"

"I don't know," I admitted. My half-empty closet stared at me. "I think I threw out most of my clothes when I was getting ready for Carla."

"Who turned out to be Carlo." Erin laughed like it was the greatest joke in the world.

"Right." I couldn't even manage a smile.

"Well, wait till you hear what I'm wearing." For the next five minutes, Erin babbled on cheerfully about a yellow miniskirt she was going to match with a black tank top and textured stockings. "What do you think?" she said finally.

"It sounds interesting," I said cautiously. A black tank top and a yellow mini! I thought she'd look like an overgrown bumblebee, but I knew that wasn't what she wanted to hear. Erin dresses for school the same way she does for rock concerts. Usually she gets away with it, but sometimes her mother catches her at the front door and makes her change.

I had just hung up the phone when my mother tapped lightly on my door.

"Don't stay up too late, honey," she said. "You'll need to leave for school a little early tomorrow."

"I will?" I reached for a bottle of frosted beige nail polish. Usually I don't bother with things like that, but as Erin said, it was The Big Day tomorrow. I'd be seeing kids I hadn't seen all summer, and I decided to go all out.

"Yes," she said breezily, looking at my dresser top, which had already returned to its naturally cluttered state. "You'll need to get Carlo to the principal's office by seven-thirty, and then to the guidance counselor by seven-forty-five."

She perched on the edge of the bed, ticking off items in a red spiral notebook. "I left his class schedule on the kitchen table, plus his lunch card, and his activity card. I've already spoken to all his teachers, so they'll be expecting him. And oh, yes, Miss Simms in the Study Center said Carlo can have a special English tutor if he needs one. He's supposed to stop by and see her at three-fifteen, and they can discuss it then." She crossed her long legs, and chewed her pencil stub thoughtfully. "I guess that's it," she said doubtfully. "Unless you can think of something I'm forgetting."

"You never forget anything," I said wryly. My mother is one of the most disgustingly organized people I know. She makes lists of household chores, lists of

Christmas ornaments and gift ideas, lists of recipes for dinner parties. She even makes lists of lists!

"Well, I want his first week to go smoothly," she said a little worriedly. "Jamie—" she got up and softly closed the door "—do you think Carlo's happy here? He seemed a little quiet at dinner."

"He's probably just tired from the sun and the swimming. I feel pretty wiped out myself." I faked a yawn, hoping she'd take the hint.

She didn't. She tucked a pillow behind her head, all set for a good, long chat. "I really want to make him feel at home. It must be tough on him, you know."

"Yes, I know. Strange country, new people, new language, none of his family around." I rattled off the list in a flat voice. By now, I had the routine down pat.

"Jamie!" She looked shocked. "You sound like you don't even like him."

I don't, I longed to say. "He's okay," I said tightly. "But he's not exactly what we expected, is he?"

"Oh, Jamie," she said, reaching over and squeezing my hand, "you really *were* counting on having a girl stay with us, weren't you?"

I nodded. "I even cleaned up my room."

Mom laughed. "The supreme sacrifice."

"Well, you know what I mean," I said defensively.

"I admit it was a bit of a surprise seeing him at the airport." She smiled at the memory. "But I think things are really going to work out well, don't you?" She glanced at me. "Michael really likes him, and it sounds like he hit it off with all your friends today." When I didn't say anything, she yawned and stood up.

"Guess I'll go to bed," she said slowly. "We've got a big show opening at Pulsations tomorrow. It's that new artist you like — the one who does all the neon sculpture."

Pulsations is this really neat art gallery where Mom works. She's assistant manager, which means she does everything from interviewing artists to displaying work. You wouldn't think it would be a big deal to hang a few pictures, but Mom insists there's an art to it. I've seen her work on the lighting for a painting for half an hour, and then change her mind and start all over.

"Maybe I'll drop by after school, after I take Carlo home," I said.

"Why don't you bring Carlo along?" she suggested enthusiastically. "We can give him a taste of American art. In fact, if you get there around four, I'll spring for some cappuccino at Giorgio's. Carlo will think he's right back in Rome."

"Wonderful," I said weakly. Why had I opened my big fat mouth? I had been looking forward to spending some time alone. Now I'd be stuck with a double dose of Carlo.

"Jamie, wake up!" my mother was saying frantically the next morning. I opened my eyes blearily, taking in her trim beige suit and cocoa-colored blouse. She was holding her car keys in one hand and a cup of coffee in the other, so she was obviously on her way to work. I turned over, and burrowed back in the covers, all set to go back to sleep. Then it dawned on me. If Mom was on her way to work, it must be late — really late! I looked at the clock and panicked. How could I have overslept on my first day of school?

My mother echoed my thought like some depressing Greek chorus. "How could you have overslept on your first day of school?" she asked reproachfully.

"Why didn't you wake me up?" I returned, scrambling out of bed. It was much too late to try to look sensational, I decided. All I could hope to do was wash my face and use a dab of lip gloss.

"I thought you were up," she said, plunking her coffee cup down on the dresser. "I heard someone in the shower."

"Carlo, no doubt," I said, annoyed.

"Yes, Carlo," she said, ignoring the dig. "Look, do you need some help? I can go in to work a few minutes late, if you need me." She threw open my closet doors, took a peek, and gave me a defeated look. "You don't even have anything to wear! Why didn't you tell me? We could have gone shopping."

"Don't worry about it, Mom." I'm not a morning person, and my brain was chugging along painfully in slow motion. "I've got everything under control."

Under control? I couldn't even remember what I had planned to wear. I leaned against the dresser, trying to get the room in focus.

"Well, if you're sure," she said gratefully, glancing at her watch. "You know how my boss is if I'm late."

"I know, you go ahead." I smiled to reassure her.

"See you at four," she said. She blew me a kiss and made a quick exit. "Be sure to watch out for Carlo."

"Don't worry. I will." Carlo. I had already forgotten that I had to drag him around with me, and the memory came stabbing back like a toothache. How could I have forgotten that for the next four months, my life would be controlled by a self-satisfied Italian creep?

The minute she was gone, I turned and stared in the mirror. A quick inventory confirmed the worst. I was a walking disaster. Pale, pasty skin, dull eyes, and that hair! It looked like it had died during the night. I yanked a brush through it, grabbed a towel, and raced to the bathroom.

I jumped in the shower, let the hot water pound on me while I counted to sixty, then ran back to my room and struggled into my best jeans. I looked in the mirror. No one in their right mind would think I looked attractive, but at least I looked alive.

I smeared lip gloss on my mouth while I scooped up five new spiral notebooks, one for each subject. Lunch card, activity card, and money. Was that everything? I wondered, tossing a ballpoint pen in my canvas shoulder bag.

Everything . . . except Carlo. I hurried into the kitchen, and found him sitting calmly by the window, sipping coffee like he had all the time in the world.

"Carlo!" I shrieked. "Get up! We have to go. We're late!"

"*Buon giorno*," he said politely. "Join me for breakfast," he added smoothly, gesturing to the coffee pot.

"We don't have time for that," I exploded. "We're late, don't you understand? Late! *Ritardo*."

I wasn't sure if that was the right word, but Carlo seemed to understand.

"Ah, *ritardo*," he said, pleased. "You speak Italian. Very nice. *Molto bene*." He grinned, making no move to get up. Instead, he looked me over from head to toe, taking in my crumpled jeans and my ancient yellow top. I knew I looked terrible, but at the moment, that was the least of my worries.

"Up, Carlo! Up!" I commanded, as if he were some stubborn circus animal. I made a move to eject him bodily from the kitchen chair, and he reluctantly struggled to his feet. I noticed he was all decked out in a salmon-colored T-shirt, with a white blazer. Very *Miami Vice*.

He took a final sip of coffee, and smoothed out a nonexistent wrinkle in his white linen pants. "Ah, you Americans, always in a hurry. You never take time to — how do you say it? Stop and smell the roses."

He smiled and shook his finger playfully under my nose.

"Carlo," I said tightly, "we have exactly

three minutes to make the bus. Three minutes, do you understand?" I tossed a lank strand of hair out of my eyes and stared at him. The seconds were ticking by relentlessly, and I could feel my heart thumping in my chest. If we missed the bus, I'd have to call Mom, and. . . . I didn't want to think about the rest.

It was obvious that Carlo had never run for a bus in his life. He's probably never run for anything in his life, I thought furiously. He drew himself up to his full height, and calmly drained his coffee cup.

"We only have three minutes? Why didn't you say so?" he said coolly. "There must be no more delay. We shall leave immediately."

He smiled, gave a deep bow, and opened the door for me.

I wanted to murder him.

Chapter 6

I watched Carlo make his way down the dingy hallway of Copley High. He strutted down the jammed corridor like he owned the planet.

"Hi, Jamie!" Sherry Mitchell hugged me, like we hadn't seen each other for a year. "Did you get too much sun yesterday?"

"No, I — "

"Well, look what happened to me," she rushed on, staring at Carlo. "I got this simply awful sunburn!" She pushed her sundress to one side to reveal a lobster-colored shoulder.

Carlo looked at it politely. "That must be painful," he said softly. "In Italy, we crush the leaves of a certain plant — " he began to say, but I cut him off.

"We're in a hurry, Carlo," I reminded him. I knew that if I heard one more word about Italy, I was going to scream.

"And you rub it on the burn," Sherry was saying encouragingly.

"Yes," he said, beaming at her. It was obvious that Carlo couldn't resist female attention. "I do not know the name in English, but maybe we can find the plant here."

"Maybe we'd better get to the principal's office," I said, dragging him away.

"See you later!" Sherry said, flashing a toothy smile. "And if you find that plant, Carlo —"

"We'll let you know!" I barked. I was beginning to feel like a drill sergeant. If only Michael still went to high school, I thought resentfully. Then *he'd* be stuck with Carlo.

"A charming girl," Carlo was saying thoughtfully.

"Who?" I answered blankly. My mind was going in a million directions at once. I knew I had to get Carlo completely settled before I could escape to my own homeroom and forget about him for a couple of hours. With any luck, I wouldn't have to see him until lunch time.

"Sherry," he said softly. "That is the same name as a wine, no?"

"No," I agreed. "I mean, yes." The day was just starting and Carlo was already driving me crazy.

* * *

Copley High is always a madhouse on the first day of school. For one thing, it's one of the biggest high schools in the county, and for another, everything is computerized, and the computers break down every September. My freshman math teacher, Mr. Williams, said it's nice to have something you can always depend on, like the birds flying south for the winter, but I'm not sure if he was kidding.

The main hall was more crowded than I could ever remember, and Carlo and I had to force our way to the office, like salmon swimming upstream. I knew I looked like a wreck, which made me feel worse. My face was shining from the heat, and my hair was hanging limply around my neck.

Carlo, on the other hand, seemed to be thriving on the noise and excitement. "Ah, this is just like a movie I saw. *Fast Times at Ridgemont High*, starring Sean Penn. Did you see that film, Jamie?" he asked earnestly. "It is about these American teenagers — "

"I saw the movie, Carlo," I said quickly. Carlo talked more than any boy I had ever met. And when he talked, he used his hands a lot, which drew some curious stares from the kids around us. Actually, it wasn't just his hands that moved. It was his whole body.

"You're leaving me *here*?" he said suddenly, when we stopped outside the principal's office.

"No, I'm *waiting* for you here," I told him. "You have to talk to Mr. Hayes — he's the principal — then I'm going to take you to the guidance counselor, then we'll find your homeroom." I mentally ticked off the list of my duties, just like my mother would do. I felt tired just thinking about them.

"Homeroom?"

"Never mind, I'll explain later," I said, gratefully ushering him inside. The main office is always about twenty degrees cooler than the classrooms, so a lot of kids try to find excuses to hang around in there.

Miss Sanderson, Mr. Hayes's assistant, does everything she can to discourage visitors, so I wasn't surprised when she glanced up from her typewriter and said briskly, "State your business."

"*Buon giorno!* Good morning!" Carlo said enthusiastically. "I am Carlo Santini, exchange student from Rome, Italy, and I am here to begin school." He gave a startled Miss Sanderson a gigantic smile, and marched around the desk to shake hands with her.

She stared at him in amazement, and I nearly burst out laughing. His smile never faltered, even though she must have eyed him for a full five seconds before she took his hand.

"Well, we're very happy to have you, Carlo," she said finally. Unless I imagined it, she had two pinpoints of color in her pale cheeks. She caught me looking at her, and said firmly, "And what is *your* business, young lady?"

Carlo put an arm around me protectively. "Ah, this is Miss Jamie Hogan, the girl that I live with."

Miss Sanderson's mouth dropped open, and I said quickly, "We're his host family. He's staying with us for the semester."

"Oh." She checked an appointment book and managed a thin smile. "Mr. Hayes will see you now," she said, swiveling out of her desk chair.

"Thank you, thank you," Carlo said, bowing to her and bestowing another movie-star smile. "I am happy to meet him."

She ushered Carlo into Mr. Hayes's office, and I heard her murmur an introduction. Then she closed the door behind her, and returned to her typewriter. "You may wait in the hall," she said coolly.

I was leaning wearily against a pillar outside the office, when Andy spotted me and sauntered over.

"How's your first day back going?" he asked, tucking a loose strand of hair behind my ear.

"Not great," I said, sneaking a worried look at the clock. I hoped that Carlo wasn't in the middle of a long story with Mr. Hayes, because we were already five minutes late for the guidance counselor.

"What's wrong, Jamie?" Andy looked concerned, and I leaned close to him so our shoulders were touching against the cool marble. I recognized the lemon after-shave I gave him for his birthday, and I smiled.

"Oh, I don't know," I said vaguely. "I overslept this morning, and the day got off to kind of a bad start."

"Want to go to the cafeteria and get a Coke or something? We've got twenty minutes before homeroom." He shifted his books to one hand, so he could sneak an arm around my waist.

"Oh, Andy, I wish I could," I said truthfully, "but I'm waiting for Carlo."

His face clouded, and I could feel the muscles in his arm tighten. "What's his problem? Can't he get to class by himself?"

I explained about all the people Carlo had to see that morning. "It would take him forever to find his way around by himself."

"That's the only way he's going to learn," Andy said curtly. I noticed he was wearing a new yellow shirt and a pair of tan cords. A couple of girls eyed him, and I reminded myself how lucky I was to be dating him.

"I know, but this is his first day," I said quietly.

"Well, I hope he can find his way around after this," he said. "After all, he's what — sixteen? He shouldn't need a baby-sitter."

Carlo emerged from the office then, and started to wind his way toward us.

"How about if we get together after school?" Andy said quickly. "I could meet you at about four."

"Andy, I'd like to, but— "

"But what?" he asked impatiently.

"I've got to meet my mother at Pulsations at four sharp. I promised."

He rolled his eyes to the ceiling. "Is Carlo going, too?"

"Well, yes, as a matter of fact — "

"I'll see you at Pulsations," Andy said firmly. "Four sharp." He glowered at Carlo, who was almost up to us, and then he melted into the throng of kids.

"A lovers' quarrel?" Carlo inquired smilingly.

Where had he heard that? I wondered. I shook my head curtly. "We're going to be late for the guidance counselor," I said sharply.

Carlo stared at me, his dark eyes

thoughtful. He threw an arm around my shoulders in a friendly way, as we battled our way back into the crowd. After we had gone a few feet, he leaned close and said reassuringly, "It will be okay. You will see."

I hadn't fooled him for a minute.

Carlo caused a sensation at lunch time, just as I had expected. Andy and I had different lunch schedules, and I found myself standing uncertainly in the cafeteria line alone with Carlo. Who would we eat with? I wondered. I looked desperately for Erin and Sherry, as we pushed our trays through the line.

Carlo lingered over each item, like he was selecting his last meal.

"Veal parmigiana?" he sniffed. "No, it is impossible. It looks like dog meat."

I tried not to laugh as the woman behind the counter glared at him.

"It says *mock* veal parmigiana," I pointed out.

"What does that mean, mock?"

I thought for a moment. It's funny how you never think about what words mean when you use them every day. "It means fake."

"Fake food?" Carlo looked horrified. "Like plastic?"

"No," I giggled. "It's food all right, but it's probably chicken, not veal. Veal is too expensive," I explained.

"In Italy, we never makes jokes about food," he said seriously. "My mother makes veal parmigiana almost every Sunday." He turned to look at me, not caring that he was holding up the line. "She starts simmering the tomato sauce right after church, and it cooks on the back of the stove for hours. Then she makes homemade pasta, sometimes rigatoni or ziti, to go with it. It takes her all day," he said proudly.

"I hope she likes to cook," I said, knowing he wouldn't catch the sarcasm.

He looked at me as if I had just said something incredibly stupid. "But of course. She is Italian," he said.

I sighed. I knew it would be pointless to argue with him.

"Hey, get a move on," a red-haired guy yelled, and Carlo looked at him coolly.

"Always in a hurry," he muttered. "What did I tell you?"

"Just choose something," I pleaded. "It all tastes the same anyway."

Carlo finally decided on a club sandwich and a Coke. He looked at my diet plate in astonishment. "Diet Delight? Why do you choose that?"

"Because — never mind," I snapped. He

looked so crushed, I relented. "I like to watch my weight," I said in a low voice. We were approaching the cashier, and I dug in my purse for my lunch card.

"What!" Carlo bellowed with laughter. "You are on a diet? But that is crazy. You are already like a pole — a stick." He took in my yellow top and jeans, shaking his head sadly.

"Thanks a lot," I hissed. "And will you please keep your voice down?" A couple of kids had already turned around and were snickering at us.

"American girls are too thin," Carlo said in that arrogant way I was beginning to recognize. "No fat on them. In Italy, we like a woman to have . . . a shape." He paused and smiled at a cute blonde girl who was choosing a dessert. "That is true, no?"

She turned to the girl next to her and they both dissolved into giggles.

"Look, Jamie, you should have dessert, like this girl does. Here, I get you one." He plunked a piece of lemon meringue pie on my tray.

"Carlo," I said warningly. We had reached the end of the line, and the cashier was drumming her fingers impatiently, waiting for my lunch card. I handed it to her and was rewarded with a scowl. "Get your card out," I hissed at Carlo, who was still staring at the blonde girl.

"Take your time," the cashier offered. She beamed at Carlo. "It's probably his first day here. I love that accent." She rolled her eyes at Carlo and he grinned appreciatively.

"*Grazie*, thank you," he said humbly. "You are a nice lady."

"You are too kind," the smiling cashier replied.

Kind, my foot! I thought angrily. He's not kind at all! I felt like shouting. He just knows how to charm anything female within a hundred yards!

"Here you are," Erin said breathlessly. She'd obviously managed to slip out of the house in her bumblebee outfit, and she slid into an empty chair next to Carlo. Sherry, looking sensational in a tomato-red sundress, was right beside her.

Within minutes, the table was swarming with girls, and Carlo was practically beside himself with delight. "*Buon giorno!* Hello! How are you!" he kept saying as I made the introductions. It seemed like the whole sophomore class had decided to join us for lunch.

"How do you like America so far?" a bubbly girl named Jennifer asked him.

"It is *magnifico*, fantastic." He smiled

at her, and she nudged her friend, who decided to take the plunge.

"How do you like American girls, Carlo?"

He beamed at me. "They are — how you say? The pits."

"What!" There was a chorus of wails around the table, and Carlo hastened to explain.

"Wait, wait, maybe I make the mistake." He turned to me and said helplessly, "I thought that Michael said your friends were the pits."

Jennifer almost died laughing, and I could feel myself flushing. Carlo grabbed my hand and said urgently, "The pits — it means the best, no?"

"No, Carlo," I said stiffly. "Don't you remember? The pits means the worst." I didn't dare meet Erin's eyes, and I could feel Sherry glaring at me across the table.

"Ah, then I make a big mistake." He slapped himself on the head. "American girls are the best in the world," he finished in a ringing voice.

"That's more like it!" Jennifer yelled.

"Well, now that we've got that settled," Sherry said smoothly, "tell us all about Rome."

Carlo was happy to oblige, and for the next half hour he managed to talk nonstop and devour his club sandwich at the same time.

I tuned out after the first few minutes, and started to daydream about Andy, wishing I could have had lunch with him. I pushed my food around on my plate, making swirls in my cottage cheese, and hiding my olives under a lettuce leaf, until I realized that Carlo was saying something to me.

"You are eating almost nothing, Jamie," he said, his voice heavy with concern. "Is something wrong?"

"No, I've, uh, just got a headache." From listening to you, I felt like adding.

He broke into a wide grin. "At least it's nothing serious," he said, relieved. "In that case," he paused, and eyed my lemon pie hungrily.

I should have known. He wasn't concerned, he was hungry! I slid the plate across the table to him. "It's all yours, Carlo," I told him.

"Are you sure?" he asked, jamming his fork into it.

"I'm positive," I said wryly. "For some reason, I seem to have completely lost my appetite."

Chapter 7

I couldn't even imagine how Carlo would react to Pulsations. As far as I'm concerned, Pulsations is the most fantastic art gallery in Westchester. The building it's in is over a hundred years old, and what makes it really unusual is that long ago it was a church. When Mom's boss, Mr. Hyatt, bought it five years ago, he left most of the original decorations in place. A lot of people are taken aback when they walk into an art gallery and see stained-glass windows and old-fashioned furniture, but I think it's great.

Carlo was stunned. I had told him a little about the place on the way over, but he was still surprised at the heavy oak doors with the lionhead knobs. He glanced up at the high bell tower and back to me.

"*Chiesa*," he said softly. "Church."

"Yes, a church. But wait till you see the

inside," I said proudly. "My mom did a lot of the interior design."

We stepped inside, and a rush of cool air greeted us. "Ah, that's better," Carlo said gratefully, taking in the gray slate floors and solid white walls. The foyer had dozens of splashy abstract paintings.

"Carrera," he said, running his hand over the creamy marble with the delicate black threads running through it. "I've been to those quarries," he said. "The finest marble in Italy."

We climbed a winding staircase to Mom's office. It used to be the choir loft, and she loves it, because she can look out over the whole gallery. She was busy editing brochures for a new show, but she looked up when she saw us.

"I'm glad you could make it," she said, standing up and swiftly hugging both of us.

"I'm happy to see where you work," Carlo said politely. "Jamie said it was fantastic, but it is even more than that." He glanced at the brass organ pipes that stretched straight up to the vaulted ceiling, and shook his head. "I am at a loss for words."

That'll be the day, I thought silently.

"Well, do you want the grand tour, or shall we go for coffee first?"

"The grand tour," Carlo said promptly.

Mom buzzed her secretary on an intercom. "Sheila, can you hold down the fort for a while?" She smiled at Carlo. "I'm showing some VIPs around."

We headed downstairs to the gallery and nearly collided with Andy, who was coming around the corner. I had completely forgotten I was supposed to meet him at four! I glanced at Mom. "I invited Andy to come see the new show, Mom. Is that okay?"

"Of course," she said. "I'm glad you could join us, Andy. I think you'll enjoy Terry Street's work. Neon always draws a good crowd."

Everyone smiled and started talking once we got to the center of Pulsations. The neon exhibit had attracted a lot of attention, just as Mom had predicted, and thirty or forty people were milling around, discussing the sculptures.

"The gallery looks great, Mom," I told her, and she squeezed my hand gratefully.

Carlo looked impressed. "Did you do all this by yourself?" he asked.

"I told you she does all the display work," I said sharply. I had to admit, I was a little awed myself. Mom had covered the walls with black burlap, and had set up overhead strobe lights in the corners. The combination of the strobes and the flashing neon sculptures made the whole scene seem unreal, like something out of a movie.

"Like a Fellini work," Carlo said under his breath, and Mom looked pleased at his comparison to the famous movie director.

"Yes, that's just the look I wanted," she said. "I wanted it to seem magical, like something out of a dream."

Andy was dangerously quiet during this whole exchange, and I sneaked a look at him. His lips were set in a thin, tight line, and I knew he was disgusted. Andy's not a big art fan to begin with, and I guess the idea of a roomful of neon lights seemed crazy to him.

"What do you think of it?" I whispered.

"What do I think of a bunch of people gawking at some light bulbs flashing on and off?" he hissed back. "I think it's crazy, that's what!"

I sighed. Andy has really strong ideas, and once he's made up his mind about something, it's almost impossible to sway him.

"What's even crazier is some guy getting paid to do this stuff." He pointed to a flashing orange sign that said JOE'S DINER. "Did he steal that or make it?" Andy asked sarcastically.

"Of course he didn't steal it." I glanced around nervously, hoping no one had overheard him. "Neon is very valuable, and it's really tough to work with."

Unfortunately, Carlo chose that moment to edge closer to us.

"So, Andy," he said in a friendly voice, "which is your favorite? I, myself, like the dragon." He pointed to a brilliant green Chinese dragon, made entirely out of neon, with fiery red eyes. "It is fabulous, no?"

"It's okay." Andy shrugged, looking as if he were bored out of his mind.

I found myself getting a little annoyed. Why had he bothered coming if he was going to be in such a bad mood? It was obvious that he wasn't thrilled to see Carlo, but that was hardly my fault. I was getting a little sick of being caught in the middle.

"Or maybe you prefer the windmill?" One of the show-stoppers was a gigantic red windmill with the words MOULIN ROUGE written above it.

We joined the crowd gathered around it and Andy looked interested. "Hey, we have a picture of that in our French book. Do you remember it, Jamie? It's some famous nightclub in France."

"It's in one of my favorite sections of Paris," Carlo said casually.

"You've been to the Moulin Rouge?" I gasped.

"Of course." He looked surprised at my

reaction. "My father brings the whole family to Paris every year for my mother's birthday. They met at the Moulin Rouge, so she has a — " he paused and groped for a word " — a special feeling for it."

"That's lovely," Mom said, overhearing the last part of our conversation. "You're quite the world traveler, Carlo," she said fondly.

An hour later, when we were settled with cups of cappuccino at Giorgio's, I thought about what Mom had said. Carlo *was* different from the rest of the kids at Copley. He spoke two foreign languages — French and English — and he'd lived all over the world. Is *that* why Andy was so annoyed with him? Could it be that he was jealous? I wasn't any fan of Carlo's, but even I could see that Andy was being a little unfair to him.

"It's too bad Andy couldn't have joined us for coffee," Mom said.

"He had to work again." Even if Andy had been free, I was pretty sure he wouldn't have come with us. He'd made it clear when he left Pulsations that he'd had enough of Carlo for a long while.

"Is he your steady?" Carlo caught me off guard, and I could feel myself blushing. Luckily Mom jumped in before I could say anything. "Why, Carlo," she teased him, "you must be using a new slang book."

"Yes. I am. Well, is he, Jamie?" He stared at me, waiting for my answer.

"I suppose he is," I said finally. "I mean, neither one of us sees anyone else." For some reason, I felt very uncomfortable talking about Andy with Carlo.

I was afraid he'd ask me some more questions, but he nodded and sipped his coffee, as if he was satisfied with my answer. Mom started talking to Carlo about Italy then, and I let my mind wander, glad to be off the hook. Before I even realized what I was doing, I found myself studying him.

He was really good-looking, I decided. Girls stared at him every place we went. The waitress at Giorgio's came by every five minutes to ask him if he wanted more coffee, and the cashier was craning her neck so far to see him, I was afraid she'd get a permanent cramp. If only he weren't so incredibly arrogant and conceited, I caught myself thinking, he'd be very appealing.

"We have many of these outdoor cafes in Rome," he said suddenly, interrupting my thoughts. "I like them very much."

"Me, too," I blurted out. I had the uncomfortable feeling that he knew I had been watching him. We were sitting at a green umbrella table outdoors on the upper level of Giorgio's, and the setting sun cast a golden glow over the office buildings around us.

"I come here for lunch sometimes," Mom said, "and it's always so relaxing, I can hardly force myself to go back to work. But before I know it, the hour's up, and it's back to the salt mine."

"Salt mine?" I saw the look on Carlo's face and laughed.

"Just an expression," I assured him. "A place where you have to work really hard."

"Oh." He smiled, and I couldn't tell if he had understood or not. "It is hard to imagine having only one hour for lunch. In Italy, we take time to enjoy life, Mrs. Hogan." He was tracing a design on the tablecloth with his fork, and his dark eyes were serious. "In my father's company, everyone takes at least two, and maybe three hours for lunch."

"Three hours!" Mom looked shocked. "My boss would have a heart attack," she explained. "What would all the customers do?"

Carlo laughed. "They would be eating lunch, too. In Rome, the shops close from one to four, so the workers can have a long lunch, and maybe a *riposo*. A nap."

"It sounds nice," Mom said wistfully, "but I don't think it would work over here. Life is too fast-paced."

"You mean Americans are too impatient," Carlo pointed out.

"You're probably right." She glanced at her watch and gasped. "Well, I didn't realize how late it was," she said, reaching for the check. "We better hurry or we'll — " She stopped and laughed. "I just proved your point, didn't I?"

"I'm afraid so." Carlo winked at me. "Your mother lives life in the fast lane, no?"

"Guilty as charged," Mom agreed. She shrugged. "Jamie's father is always telling me to slow down, but there's just so much to do."

"What do you have to do right this minute?" he demanded.

She bit her lip and thought. "Well, right now I have to go to the market, and then race home and cook dinner for everybody. Then after dinner, I have to — "

"Wait, wait," Carlo said, holding up his hand. "I have a better idea."

"You do?" She handed some money to the waitress who magically appeared at her elbow, still smiling at Carlo.

"I do." He put an arm around each of us as we walked to Mom's car. "Tonight, I fix the dinner, and you, Mrs. Hogan, can relax!"

Carlo's dinner was more than a meal; it was a drama.

"I hope this works," he said, dubiously punching buttons on the microwave. He had carefully hung his blazer over a kitchen chair, and had rolled up his shirt-sleeves to his elbows. "Spaghetti sauce is supposed to simmer for three hours."

"But the microwave speeds everything up, Carlo. It cooks things differently, with rays, I think."

"Food cooked by rays," I heard him mutter, as he sliced tomatoes and red onions for a salad. "Just like science fiction. . . ."

I just smiled. "If you need some help, I could cut up some lettuce for you," I offered.

"Cut lettuce?" He looked at me as if I were insane. "You have to tear it, gently, like this." He demonstrated by delicately shredding a lettuce leaf.

"What difference does it make?"

"It ruins it if you cut it."

"But that's crazy." I laughed. "It tastes just the same whether you cut it or tear it."

Then Carlo made one of his favorite pronouncements. He drew himself up to his full height, his dark eyes flashing. "But then it would not be Italian."

"Oh, I see." I turned away so he wouldn't see me smiling. "Well, at least let me slice some of these onions for you." I took a paring knife and began whacking away at a large Bermuda onion.

"No, no!" Carlo wailed like he was in pain. "You mustn't slash the onion. The slices have to be thin, so thin you can see through them."

"Honestly, Carlo." I was running out of patience. "I think you're making too big a deal of this."

There was a hissing noise, and we both turned in time to see the big spaghetti pot boiling over.

"*Mamma mia*," Carlo whispered, raising his eyes to the ceiling. "This is the last thread!"

"Straw," I corrected him, stifling a giggle.

"Whatever," he retorted. "Now, *basta*! Enough!" He ushered me into the den. "Read a book, watch the television. Do anything you want. But stay out of my way and let me cook!"

"I hope you know what you're doing." I sighed.

"Hah!" he said, stung. "Wait till you taste. Then you know!"

Chapter 8

"He cooked spaghetti for you?" Sherry Mitchell whispered a couple of days later in awestruck tones. "Oh, I would die. I would just die!"

I gave her a disgusted look and went back to my over-cooked cheeseburger. Erin says the cook at Copley must be a vegetarian because the meat — any meat — is always charred beyond recognition.

The three of us — Erin, Sherry, and myself — were sitting at a corner table in the crowded cafeteria. Carlo couldn't join us because he had to visit the guidance counselor at twelve sharp, but he was certainly with us in spirit. Sherry couldn't stop talking about him.

"How was it?" Erin asked. I glanced at her, and could feel the corners of my mouth start to twitch. She had managed to slip out of the house wearing another unbelievable outfit, and was sporting a huge sweat shirt that she'd spatter-painted herself at a nearby boutique. No one had the nerve to criticize her artwork.

"How was what?" I felt silly talking to her Stevie Wonder sunglasses, but I resisted the impulse to tell her so.

"The spaghetti," she said impatiently. Erin may be an idiot about boys, but she's always very practical about food. "Did he teach you some great new Italian recipe?"

"Erin, you know I'm not into cooking, but. . . ."

"But . . ." she prompted.

I gave up on the cheeseburger and pushed my plate aside. "I have to admit it was very good." I smiled, remembering how upset he'd been with the microwave. "He made something called spaghetti Milanese, but it took him forever. And you should have seen the kitchen — it looked like he'd just fixed Thanksgiving dinner for thirty people. There were dirty dishes everywhere. The sink was piled high with them."

"That sounds wonderful," Sherry said brightly. I thought she'd lost her mind, but I could only focus on her next words: "Hi there, Carlo. We were just talking about you."

"Ah, you were saying something good, I hope." Carlo grinned and slid into the seat next to me. He had dressed carefully for his interview with the counselor, and was wearing a pair of ivory linen slacks with a black silk shirt. He looked like he belonged on the streets of Rome instead of in a school in Westchester County, but I didn't have the heart to tell him.

"How did your meeting with Mr. Byer go?"

"Very good." He grinned and sneaked one of my French fries. "I think I am being excused from world history — if I am lucky."

"How come?" Erin asked, envious. "That's a required course."

"I'm taking a test on it, instead. If I do well, they give me the credit. I take it this Saturday afternoon."

"That's great, Carlo," I told him.

"Only really smart kids get credit by examination," Sherry told him seriously.

Carlo shrugged. "I have already taken world history in Italy — when I was a freshman," he added. "Our classes are more advanced than yours, I think."

I rolled my eyes, and Erin grinned. Whenever Carlo compared America to Italy, we came in a poor second.

"What are you guys doing this weekend?" Sherry asked coyly. I had the feeling she was leading up to something, and I was determined to stop her cold.

"I've got a date with Andy," I said quickly. "For once, he doesn't have to work at Pappy's." I hadn't seen Andy since the disastrous day at Pulsations, and I could hardly wait to go out with him.

"And I'm going out with Jeff," Erin said happily. "We're going to see a double horror feature at the Colony Drive-In. How about you, Sherry? What are you and Kurt up to?"

"Nothing," Sherry answered in a glum voice. She was looking right at Carlo, and I groaned inwardly. I couldn't believe it! She was making a play for my houseguest!

"Kurt's parents are going out of town to visit some aunt who's about a million years old, and they're making Kurt go with them." She borrowed Erin's Coke and took a noisy sip. "Have you ever heard of anything so boring in your life?"

"Family is very important," Carlo said sternly. "I have many aunts and uncles who are too old to come into town. My father takes us out to the country every Sunday after lunch to visit them. We never miss a single week."

"Oh, Carlo," Sherry said laughing, "sometimes I can't believe you're for real! You're so old-fashioned."

"I don't think having respect for your

family is old-fashioned," Carlo said stiffly.

"Hey, don't get mad." Sherry realized she had gone too far, and was instantly apologetic. "I think it's kind of cute. It's just that in America, well, we don't make such a big deal about relatives, do we?" When nobody said anything, she turned the corners of her mouth down playfully, like some spoiled little kid.

"Anyway," she went on, "I'm going to be all alone this weekend, while you guys are out having fun." She let her voice trail off while she looked steadily at Carlo.

Erin got the point before Carlo did. "Hey, I've got a great idea, Sherry. Why don't you come to the movies with us Saturday night? And you, too, Carlo. It'll be fun."

It's too bad they'd already handed out this year's Academy Awards because Sherry did a really good job of looking surprised. "I never thought of that," she gushed. "I'd love to go! How about it, Carlo?"

"Of course, I would be honored to take you," he said gallantly. "And you, Jamie, will you and your friend Andy be there, also?"

"I don't think — " I began, but Erin cut me off.

"You bet they will," she promised. "We'll

take Jeff's van and stock it with plenty of food and soda." She was grinning from ear to ear, her eyes masked by the ridiculous sunglasses. "Just think, this will be Carlo's first drive-in movie."

"I should check with Andy," I said in a low voice, but Erin shook her head vigorously.

"Don't be silly. He's going to *love* the idea!"

"I hate the idea! I can't believe you agreed to it," Andy said later that day.

"Well, you see, Erin said that she and Jeff were going, and then Sherry said she had nothing to do because Kurt was going to be out of town."

"And then the next thing you know, *we* were invited," he added angrily.

"Something like that." Andy and I were standing in the hall between classes, and we practically had to shout to hear each other over the noise.

"I still don't know why you agreed to go. Why didn't you just say no?" he asked.

"I don't know," I said helplessly. Someone slammed a locker door right next to me and I jumped. "I thought it might be fun."

He gave me one of those intense glares that only brown-eyed people can manage.

"And I couldn't think of how to get out of it. It would have looked funny to say no."

"I thought so," he said disgustedly. "Jamie, I was counting on being *alone* with you tomorrow night. We haven't seen each other in a long time. . . ."

"I know. You've been busy working," I reminded him.

"And you've been busy with that Italian guy." He couldn't even bring himself to say Carlo's name.

I wanted to point out that if I hadn't been spending time with Carlo I would have been sitting home twiddling my thumbs, but I didn't think this was the right time to antagonize him. "My mother likes me to spend time with him."

"Humpf! She babies him. That's the whole problem."

I shifted my books to one arm and leaned back against the cold tile wall. "This won't go on forever, Andy. I just have to hang out with him until he gets settled— until he makes his own friends."

"That may *never* happen," Andy said dryly. He gave a short laugh. "He's not exactly Mr. Congeniality, is he?"

"Well, *my* friends like him," I said hesitantly.

"Your *girl* friends," he sneered.

"Haven't you noticed the guys avoid him like the plague? Have you ever wondered about that?"

I thought of Sherry's pronouncement at the beach: They're all jealous.

"I suppose you're right," I said, wanting to end the argument. As usual, I was caught in the middle.

I had just walked in the door from school on Friday when Mom called me from work.

"I've done an incredibly stupid thing," she wailed. "I left all my notes on Robert Henderson on the dresser, and I'm doing an interview with him at five."

"Do you want me to bring them down to you?" I looked at my watch. "I can catch the three-thirty bus."

"How about Michael giving you a ride?"

Michael slammed his books on the kitchen table just then, and I grabbed his arm. "Perfect timing," I assured her. "He just walked in. We'll see you in fifteen minutes."

"You saved my life," she said gratefully and hung up.

We were already in the car when Michael spotted Carlo walking up the driveway.

"Hey, Carlo," he called cheerfully, "want to go for a ride with us? We have to go down to Pulsations."

"He probably has things to do," I whispered hopefully, but it was too late. Carlo bounded over to the car like a happy puppy, and jumped in the backseat.

I sighed and stared straight ahead. It was useless to fight it. Carlo was destined to be my constant companion, no matter what I said or did.

Pulsations usually closes at five on Fridays, but Mom often stays late to catch up on paperwork or to talk to artists. She was hunched over her typewriter when we came in, but she stood up when she spotted us.

"Everybody's gone for the day, and Mr. Henderson should be here any minute. Do you think you can keep yourselves occupied while I interview him? It should only take half an hour."

"Of course. We can take another look around — " Carlo broke off suddenly and stared at the pipe organ in the corner of the loft. "I would love to play this," he said, gently lifting the lid. "It is permitted?"

"You want to play the organ?" Mom said doubtfully. "Carlo, the thing's probably been here for a hundred years. No one touches it, so I'm sure it's out of tune." She glanced at the grimy brass pipes that stretched to the ceiling.

"But you don't object?"

"No, of course not," she said warmly. "Play to your heart's content, Carlo, but don't expect miracles. Probably half the keys don't work." The front door bell chimed and Mom headed for the stairs. "That must be him. See you guys later," she tossed over her shoulder.

"You're really going to play that?" I asked incredulously.

"Of course. I love organ music." Carlo gently lifted the wooden lid, and ran his hands lightly over the yellowed keys. He tried a few of the stops, and nodded, satisfied. "Everything seems to work. You know, Jamie, there is an organ just like this at my uncle's church in Tuscany. He's a pastor at a very small country church," he explained. "When I used to visit him in the summer, I would stay up half the night playing fugues."

"Fugues?"

Carlo smiled. "Don't you say fugue in English? Bach, Handel, Mendelssohn . . . all the great composers wrote them."

"You *like* classical music?" I was surprised.

He nodded. "I like all kinds of music. Classical, religious, rock, jazz." He swiveled around on the stool to face me. "Don't you?"

"Well, I'm really not into classical

music," I hedged. That was the understatement of the year. I was still trying to figure out what a fugue was.

"Listen," he said, and he brought his hands down on the keys. A fantastic sound filled the gallery, and I could feel a shiver go right down to my toes. His fingers moved slowly, surely over the keys, and I recognized the opening bars of a familiar melody.

"Beethoven?" I asked hesitantly.

"Very good," he teased me. "The Fifth Symphony — that's the one everybody knows."

"That's the *only* one I know," I admitted meekly.

"Why do you like it?" he asked suddenly. I noticed he played like he was in a world of his own.

"I don't know," I said. "I'm not used to figuring out why I like something."

"Well, think about it," he encouraged me.

"Let's see. . . ." I squinted my eyes shut and I could practically feel the music pulsing inside me. "It's mysterious," I said finally. "And powerful."

"Yes, very powerful," he said softly.

"And there's something, I don't know, something wonderful about it," I told him. "It's like the music is inside me, and yet it fills the whole room."

"That's the way music is supposed to make you feel, Jamie."

He played for an hour altogether then, and I was really disappointed when Mom appeared, saying that she'd enjoyed the concert but that it was time to leave. I hated to have the moment end, and I'm not sure if it was because I fell in love with the music or if it was because I was seeing another side of Carlo.

I tried to figure it out on the way home, and I couldn't. Somehow Carlo seemed different when he was playing the organ. Not arrogant and conceited the way he usually did, just very likable. Or was it just *my* reaction to him that was different?

The phone was ringing when we opened the door and I snatched it off the hook.

It was Andy, and he sounded annoyed. "Where have you been?" he demanded irritably.

"I, uh, had to do an errand for my mother." I didn't want to tell him that I had been listening to Carlo play classical music on a hundred-year-old organ. He'd think I was out of my mind. "Why, what's up?" I asked, curious.

"Mr. Androtti told me I could come in a little late tonight," he sighed, "so I was going to spend a couple of hours with you.

It's too late now," he added reproachfully.

"I'm sorry," I said lamely. I lowered my voice, conscious of Mom bustling around the kitchen, and Carlo standing just a few feet away. "It would have been fun to see you."

"What? I can't hear you," he complained.

"I said I'll see you tomorrow," I said hastily. "The drive-in movie, remember?"

"Oh, that," he said glumly. "I wish it was going to be just the two of us, Jamie."

"It'll be fun," I said gamely. Carlo was pretending to read the paper but I knew he was listening to every word. "You know what they say," I added. "The more the merrier."

When Andy didn't answer, I put the receiver very close to my lips and blew a kiss into the phone. "See you tomorrow, Andy," I said softly.

I hung up feeling vaguely uneasy. Something was wrong, and I couldn't put my finger on it. Carlo caught my eye and smiled then, and I suddenly realized what it was: I was *glad* that he was coming to the drive-in with us!

Knowing this didn't make me feel any better, though. It just made me realize how really confused my feelings were.

Chapter 9

Maybe it was too chilly a night to go to a drive-in. The temperature had dropped suddenly during the day, and gusts of cold air swirled around our feet. Or maybe we should have brought cheese and fruit, instead of greasy bags of chips and pretzels. Or maybe Italians just don't appreciate Godzilla movies.

Anyway, the "triple date" was definitely a mistake. About halfway through the first feature, I stole a look at Carlo, who was crunched up in the corner of Jeff's beat-up van. A giggling Sherry was next to him and the two of them could have modeled for those comedy-and-tragedy masks they use in Greek theater. Sherry was smiling from ear to ear, having the time of her life, and Carlo's frown was getting deeper by the minute.

I sighed and passed him some Doritos.

"Are you hungry, Carlo?" I whispered. The darkness seemed to swallow up my words, and I had to lean close and repeat them. "We've got some more drinks back here. I think there's root beer, and cream soda."

He shook his head. "No, thanks," he said briefly. He gave me a pained look, and made a feeble effort to stretch his legs.

Sherry's eyes were glued raptly to the screen, and suddenly she squealed in terror as Godzilla flattened a whole city block. "Oh, I can't watch," she said, burying her face in Carlo's eggshell-colored blazer. "Tell me when the scary part's over." She glanced at him from under her lids. I thought she was overdoing the panic bit, myself. I happened to know for a fact that she had seen *Godzilla Meets Megalon* three times, and she had never been terror-stricken before.

I caught Carlo's eye and he smiled weakly. A martyr's smile, not his usual flash of dazzling teeth. Poor Carlo, I found myself thinking. This isn't his idea of a great evening. For some reason, I remembered the way he had looked playing the organ at Pulsations — his eyes dreamy as his fingers had moved over the keys.

Andy squeezed my arm urgently, jolting me back to the present. "You're missing the best part of the movie," he said insistently. I glanced at the screen in time to see Megalon devouring Tokyo. Thousands of people hurtled through the streets, as the monster snapped towering office buildings in half like they were toothpicks.

I stifled a yawn, and caught myself sneaking another look at Carlo. He looked unbelievably bored. And very handsome. The flickering light was playing over his face, making interesting shadows over his high cheekbones. His dark eyes were unreadable. He turned slowly and looked at me. For a brief moment, our eyes caught and held.

I felt a strange tugging at my heart, and I looked away. Something funny was going on, and it took me a few minutes to figure out what it was. Then it dawned on me. For the first time since I had met him, I was seeing Carlo as a boy! And not just any boy, but a wonderful boy. A boy that I could become interested in.

I could feel the adrenalin racing through my veins in that fight-or-flight reaction we learned about in biology class. My choice was clear: flight!

"Andy, let's get some popcorn," I said suddenly. I stood up quickly, and almost banged my head on the ceiling.

"Hey, what's the rush?" Andy complained. He was eating fistfuls of pretzels while Megalon dive-bombed a whole army.

"I just want to get some fresh air," I said weakly. I could feel Carlo's eyes on me, very dark and intense.

"Ouch!" Andy yelled excitedly. "Direct hit!"

The action on the screen had captivated him. "Please, Andy," I began, but it was no use. I couldn't compete with Megalon, who was methodically popping people in his mouth like they were salted peanuts.

"I'll be right back," I muttered. I slid open the rusty door to the van, and stepped out into the crisp night air. I started walking quickly toward the concession stand, ignoring catcalls from some boys in a yellow convertible.

"Hey, honey, where are you going?" one of them yelled.

"Nowhere," I said sharply. That was partly true. I didn't care where I went. I just knew I had to get away from the van, away from the thoughts that were spinning in my head. Was I getting interested in Carlo? What was wrong with me?

"Jamie?" The voice was low, hesitant, and I stopped in my tracks. I spun around just as Carlo touched my elbow. "You shouldn't be out here alone," he said softly. "Some of the people here" — he glanced at the yellow convertible — "their manners are not the best, no?"

"I guess not," I agreed. "But I'll be okay. Go on back — you're missing the movie," I reminded him.

He laughed, and said, "No problem. I'm not missing much. Like you Americans say, when you've seen one monster movie, you've seen them all."

"That's not completely true," I said, smiling at him. He took my arm as we headed for the popcorn stand.

"No? The good monster will win, the bad monster will lose. It is the American way," he said teasingly.

We ordered Cokes and popcorn, and waited side by side under the brightly lit awning.

"But there are all different kinds of monsters," I said, continuing the conversation. "There's Godzilla and King Kong and Radon and Mothra — "

"Mothra?" Carlo interrupted.

"He was a giant moth. You see, he started out as a giant caterpillar and then he evolved." I started to explain Mothra's history, but I found myself laughing. Monster movies sound really crazy if you try to describe them in logical terms.

"Ah, I understand. *Metamorphosi.*"

"Metamorphosi?" I struggled with the unfamiliar word. "Oh, yes," I said, understanding "Metamorphosis."

He nodded politely and paid for the popcorn and drinks. We started to walk back to the car, and then Carlo said suddenly, "The night sky is so beautiful. Do you think we could sit at one of those tables for a few minutes?" He gestured to a cluster of wrought-iron tables and chairs hidden under some weeping willow trees.

"Uh, sure," I stammered. What would Sherry think? For that matter, what would Andy think? I only hesitated for a moment, and then I followed Carlo to the tables. After all, there was nothing wrong with getting a breath of fresh air, was there? And I *had* asked Andy to come with me. . . .

"This is better," Carlo said firmly, easing himself into a wrought-iron chair. We sipped our drinks silently for a moment, listening to an owl hooting somewhere in the distance.

"These chairs aren't very comfortable," I said, shifting my weight on the narrow metal seat.

Carlo laughed. "No, but it's an improvement. At least, I have a seat to myself."

I flushed, remembering how close Sherry had sat next to him in the van. "Sherry gets a little carried away," I said, not wanting to be disloyal to one of my friends.

He didn't answer, and was staring intently at the sky. "Look, there's Cassiopeia," he said quietly.

"You know the constellations?" I asked, surprised.

"Many of them." He didn't take his eyes off the sky. "When I was very young, my father bought me a book about the stars. We have a country house, and I used to sleep outside on summer nights. I'd curl up in a sleeping bag and stare at the sky for hours." He leaned to one side and pointed through the trees. "You can see Gemini and Hydra."

I squinted in the direction he was pointing. "I'm no good at picking out stars," I said apologetically. "I can't even spot the obvious ones."

"Sure you can." He got up and crouched down next to me. "Look where I'm pointing." He lifted my chin very gently, and traced an outline in the sky. "Seven Sisters — that's the easiest of all, because the stars are clustered together, just like a family." I followed his lead, and suddenly I saw them — a handful of diamonds nestled together in a black-velvet sky.

"Now I see it," I said excitedly.

"And Serpens Caput."

"Serpens? A snake, right?"

"Right." He nodded, pleased. "If you look carefully, you can see the head and the tail. It's easy to pick out the animal constellations." I looked carefully, and finally recognized a snake-like creature winding its way across an inky landscape.

"It takes a little imagination to see it as a snake," I protested.

"But of course," he said teasingly. "That's why it's so much fun. If it was easy, there would be no challenge." He paused, scanning the sky. "Do you know Canis Minor?"

I struggled to make the connection. "Canis. That means dog, doesn't it?"

"It does," he said, craning his neck to see. "And there it is. You can't miss it."

I stood up to get a better look, and before I knew what was happening, Carlo's arm was wound around my waist. He was leaning very close, pointing to a blob that vaguely resembled a dog. At least I think it resembled a dog. To be honest, I wasn't thinking very clearly at the moment. Maybe it was the tingling night air, or maybe it was Carlo's closeness, but all of a sudden, I could feel my cheeks flaming. He's not at all almost like a sister, I thought.

I pulled away, embarrassed, and said

shakily, "Maybe we'd better get back now. They'll be wondering what happened to us."

Carlo gave me a funny look, and slowly dropped his arm. "Yes, maybe we'd better," he said in that engaging voice. "We can look at the stars another time." He smiled. "We've barely scratched the surface, Jamie. We haven't covered Gemini or Andromeda or Leo. And we can't forget Taurus and Ursa Minor."

"No, we certainly can't miss any of those," I said, trying for a light touch. Look at the stars another time? He must be kidding! I turned and walked swiftly back to the van, making my mind a blank. Something really strange was happening between me and Carlo, something I wouldn't even let myself think about.

"What do you mean you were looking at the stars?" Andy said suspiciously. "You were gone for nearly half an hour."

"Well, I know, but Carlo wanted to show me how to identify the constellations. He really knows a lot about them," I said brightly.

Andy looked unimpressed. It was nearly midnight, and we were sitting on the porch swing. Jeff had dropped us off with Carlo half an hour ago, and after saying a quick good-night to Sherry, Carlo had disappeared inside.

"It's not much fun being dumped by your girl friend at a drive-in," Andy complained, determined to continue the argument. "You should have heard the jokes Jeff and Erin were making. Sherry was furious."

"What kind of jokes?" I tucked my legs under me and rested my head on Andy's shoulder. Usually I can charm Andy out of his bad moods by holding his hand, or touching him on the shoulder, but tonight nothing seemed to work. It was almost as though he was determined to have a fight with me.

"Can't you guess?" he asked coldly.

Actually, I could, but I wasn't going to let him know that. "No, I can't," I said with more assurance than I felt. "I don't know what you're talking about."

He gave a heavy sigh and stared sulkily out at the darkness. "I don't want to draw you a picture, Jamie," he said wearily, "but if you insist. . . ." He turned to look at me then, but I kept my face expressionless.

"Well?" I questioned.

"They said you'd probably start dating him."

"What? Date him?" I tried a laugh, but

it came out forced. "Well, honestly, Andy, what's the big fuss about? They were kidding, that's all. Date Carlo? That'll be the day." I glanced at the house and lowered my voice. "You know the two of us aren't the greatest pals in the world. I told you that he gets on my nerves. In fact, he drives me crazy."

"I know he used to," Andy said hesitantly. "But lately, I'm beginning to wonder if maybe you're changing your mind about him." He paused and stared at his hands as though he had never seen them before. "Look, this is really hard for me to say, but I had the idea that maybe — "

"Maybe what?" I stood up slowly and wandered over to the porch railing. My heart was hammering away in my chest, and I could feel my knees trembling.

"That maybe you really like the guy," he said flatly.

There was this awful silence, and I gripped the wooden railing as hard as I could.

I felt this terrible lump in my throat, and I didn't even understand why. "Andy," I started to say, but I couldn't get any further because he suddenly jumped up and covered the distance between us and put his arms around me.

"It's not like you think with Carlo," I

told him finally. "I spend time with him because I *have* to, that's all. My mother expects me to."

"Are you sure that's all there is to it?"

I nodded, and he hugged me tightly. "Jamie," he said slowly. "I don't want anyone to come between us."

"Of course not," I said, hugging him back.

He looked directly into my eyes. "You mean that?"

"I do," I insisted.

At the moment, I really meant it.

Chapter 10

It was Erin who had to spell it out for me. We were shopping for jeans one night in late October when she decided to lay it on the line.

"You know what the whole problem is? You have a crush on Carlo, and you won't admit it to yourself." She turned slowly in front of the three-way mirror and tugged at the waistband on a pair of size-five Levis. "Too tight?" Her eyes met mine in the mirror.

"Yes. No. I don't know." I bit my lip and jumped to my feet. "Look, Erin, do you think we can go now? I'm just not in the mood for shopping."

"I knew it. That's the first sign of a crush," she said.

"Don't be silly." I tucked a strand of hair back in my ponytail and zipped up my windbreaker. "I'm not the type to get a crush on a guy. Plus I've got Andy, remember?"

Erin nodded seriously. "Exactly. That's why you feel so guilty. You've fallen for Carlo, and you don't know what to do about it."

I laughed a little nervously as she wriggled out of the jeans and grabbed her purse. "I don't feel guilty. Just confused."

"Don't be confused. Why can't you trust your feelings, like everyone else?" She handed the jeans to the cashier and looked at me. "Have you kissed him yet?"

"Erin!" I looked to see if the cashier had heard her. "What a thing to say!"

"Don't tell me you haven't thought about it." She sighed and rolled her eyes. "Living in the same house with him, *anybody* would think about it. Anybody!"

"Yeah, well, he's just a . . . a guest as far as I'm concerned. And anyway, he'll be going back to Italy in eight more weeks." Eight weeks! I felt a pang as I said it.

Erin tucked the shopping bag under her arm and headed for the revolving door. "So it would be crazy to like him, wouldn't it?"

"Completely crazy."

"And after all, you already have a boyfriend."

"Exactly."

She shoved open the glass door and a blast of cold air hit us. "So you're just going to let Carlo go back to Italy and you'll never think about him, or wonder what might have been."

I took a deep breath. "That's right."

There was a long pause while we walked to the bus stop. "Well, I'm certainly glad *that's* settled."

"So am I."

I ignored her mischievous smile.

During the next few weeks, Carlo was very busy with school work and I was secretly pleased that we weren't thrown together as much. I didn't really understand what had happened that night at the drive-in, but I had no intention of letting history repeat itself. The boy-girl relationship that Andy suspected — and Erin teased me about — never materialized.

Until a day in mid-November.

It was eight o'clock on a Saturday morning, and Carlo was sitting in the kitchen, scanning *The New York Times*. I cracked open a tube of frozen crescent rolls and was about to pop them in the oven when I heard Carlo exclaim, *"Mamma mia,* a Fellini movie festival. What I would give to go to that!"

"A Fellini festival?" I said politely. I stifled a yawn and poured a cup of tea. I handed Carlo a mug of instant coffee — he had finally given up on finding freshly brewed espresso — and sat down next to him. "Where is it?"

"In Manhattan," he said, pointing to a column in the entertainment section. "Do you like Fellini?"

"Sure," I said agreeably. "I mean, I think so."

Carlo continued to talk about Fellini. "He is a true hero in my country!" He gave me a wistful smile. "I don't suppose there is any way we could go. . . ."

"To Manhattan?" Dad called from the den. "Of course you can go. I'd been meaning to take you there, anyway, Carlo." He wandered out to the kitchen and stared at the newspaper. "I've got to work today, but you could take him into the city, Jamie."

"Well, I don't know if I can," I said hesitantly. "I said I'd help Mom today."

"Oh, we can catch up on things next week," Mom said cheerfully.

"See, it's all settled," Dad said. He opened his wallet and handed me some folded bills. "You kids have some fun. Take Carlo around, show him the town, on the house." He smiled at Carlo. "Jamie knows New York like the back of her hand, Carlo. We used to go there every Sunday when she and Michael were little. SoHo, Greenwich Village, Fifth Avenue, she'll take you everywhere, won't you, honey?"

"Of course," I said, managing a tight smile.

"*Buono!*" Carlo said happily. "We will spend the whole day together."

"*Buono*," I muttered. What was I getting myself into?

"Fifth Avenue," Carlo sighed ecstatically three hours later. "It's the Champs-Elysees of Paris and the Via Veneto of Rome all rolled into one, no?"

"I guess so. I've never seen those streets, so I don't know how to compare them." We had just taken a brisk walk through Central Park and were heading south on Fifth Avenue, past all the huge buildings and chic stores. Carlo stopped briefly to look at a solid chocolate Ferrari in a fancy chocolate-shop window. He pointed to the price tag, and whistled softly.

"New York is expensive," I agreed. "But you can still get some bargains."

"Yes?"

"Yes," I said firmly. "If you feel like walking about twenty blocks, I'll take you to Macy's."

"Ah, I have heard of Macy's. A giant department store, no?"

"A giant department store, yes."

Carlo was as excited as a little kid on Christmas Day in Macy's. I took him to the electronics department where he delighted the customers by playing the opening bars of a Beethoven sonata on a synthesizer.

"Listen to the sounds this can make, Jamie!" He flipped a switch on the synthesizer and a heavy rock beat thumped through the display area. Carlo ran his fingers lightly over the keyboard, playing the old Beatles song, "Yesterday," while I listened in awe. Then he pushed a button marked VIOLINS and slid into another Beatles favorite, "Strawberry Fields."

"Magnifico," he muttered. He seemed oblivious to the crowd that had gathered around the counter, and was totally lost in the music. He looked sensational in a navy sweater and tan pants, and several girls were eyeing him. There was something magnetic about Carlo, no doubt about it. I remembered that afternoon in Pulsations and started to feel a little edgy.

"Uh, maybe we'd better look at a few more things, and then move on, Carlo," I prompted him. "If you want to catch that film festival, we'll have to hurry."

"Yes, you're right," he said apologetically. He turned off the synthesizer and beamed at the salesman. *"Grazie,"* he said gratefully. "Wonderful machine.

"When I play music, I get carried away," he said, as we made our way to the escalator. "You must always remember to stop me. I get caught up in the magic."

I nodded, and tried to look indifferent. I certainly wasn't going to admit that Carlo's music had a magical effect on me, too!

"I didn't know there were places like this in New York," Carlo said later that evening. We had spent most of the afternoon at the Fellini film festival, and were having an early supper before taking the train back to Westchester.

I had picked a small French restaurant that I thought Carlo would like. It was very dim inside, and the brick walls were lined with modern art.

"I'm glad you like it." We were sitting at a tiny corner table, with one perfect rose in a silver bud vase in the center of it.

Carlo had spoken to the waitress in French, and I asked him about it afterward. "You speak French fluently, don't you?" I said, impressed. I remembered all too well how I had struggled with the terrors of the subjunctive tense.

"Not fluently," he said modestly. "Enough to get around in Paris." He made a seesaw motion with his hands. "I speak French and German about the same. My English is maybe a little better."

"You speak German, too?"

I must have looked amazed because Carlo smiled. "Jamie, most Europeans speak several languages. I am not unusual, believe me."

"You're *very* unusual," I insisted. I realized too late it was the wrong thing to say, because something really amazing happened: Carlo reached right across the table and took my hand!

"You think so?" he asked. "I think *you* are the one who is unusual. And very special." His fingers tightened around my hand, and I could feel my face getting hot.

I stared at our entwined hands on the pale blue tablecloth, and wondered what to do next. There was a very long pause, and I knew I had to say something to break the silence. "Oh no, not at all. I'm not special." I tripped over the words like I was speaking a foreign language.

"Why do you say that?" he murmured.

I managed to tear my eyes away from our clasped hands to look at Carlo. "Well, uh, for one thing, I barely got through French 101," I said a little breathlessly. Carlo was still holding my hand, and I had no idea how to retrieve it.

Carlo smiled and edged his chair a little closer to mine. "I don't mean you're special because you speak foreign languages, Jamie." His dark eyes were very intense, and he gave my hand a little squeeze. "I'm trying to say that you're the most terrific person I've ever met."

I stared helplessly at him. My mind was a blank, and I was at a total loss for words. Was Carlo saying what I thought he was saying?

"Carlo," I said unsteadily, "I think you're a terrific person, too, but — "

"But what, *cara*?" he asked softly.

A warning bell rang through my brain. *Cara* meant dear, or darling. "But our dinner's here," I said brightly, just as the waitress put two steaming dishes in front of us.

"How can I thank you for such a wonderful day?" Carlo said sincerely several hours later. The lights were dimmed in the train car, and I stared out the darkened window as we wound our way out of Manhattan toward Westchester.

"It was fun for me, too, Carlo," I said truthfully. "You know so much about art and music and films."

"But you taught me about subways and synthesizers," he said, touching the tip of my nose. He smiled at me.

I could feel my cheeks getting hot, and I stared out the window again so he wouldn't notice. But he was too quick for me, and gently turned my chin so I had to face him.

121

"What is it outside that holds your attention?"

"Nothing, I — " I started to say. I never finished the sentence, though, because Carlo suddenly bent his head and kissed me! I pulled back, and the two of us stared at each other. Then he kissed me again, very gently, and laid his cheek against mine. I couldn't resist, and I snuggled against him.

"Jamie," he whispered. "I've wanted to spend a day like this with you ever since we met."

"You have?" I managed to say. My heart was thumping like a tom-tom in my chest, and it was difficult to speak.

"Yes," he answered. "But I knew I'd have to be very patient and not rush you." He chuckled. "You weren't too thrilled with me in the beginning."

"I thought you'd be a girl," I protested. "I was disappointed, that's all."

"And what do you think now?"

"I'm . . . I'm glad you're a boy," I said honestly.

He chuckled softly and I smiled in his arms. Glad he's a boy? As Erin would say, that has got to be the understatement of the year!

Then a sobering thought hit me. What would I tell Erin? And even worse, what would I tell Andy?

Chapter 11

"I knew it, I knew it, I knew it!" Erin said the next day. She was so excited, I could hardly understand her. "Oh, it's so romantic! Didn't I tell you this would happen?" she demanded. "It was just *meant* to be! It was, like, written in the stars, you know?"

I shifted the phone to my other ear and glanced at the clock. It was almost nine on a Sunday morning, and I could hear someone making breakfast in the kitchen. Carlo, perhaps? I thought of our train ride last night, and wanted to rush into the kitchen and give him a big hug.

"There is one problem, you know," I said quietly. "Andy." I paused. "What am I going to do?"

Her tone immediately changed. "I don't think you should handle it over the phone. When are you going to see him again?" Erin said practically.

"Today at two. We're going for a walk in the park, and then, I don't know. I thought I'd invite him back for supper."

"I'd definitely settle things today, if I were you. It's not going to be easy, but the quicker you get everything out in the open, the better." Then she said hesitantly, "Do you think he suspects anything?"

"I'm afraid so." I told her what he'd said after the drive-in movie.

"Well, it won't be so much of a shock, then, will it?" she said cheerfully.

"Erin, it's still going to be tough on him." I felt awful just thinking about Andy.

"*Que sera, sera . . .*" she said gaily. "You know, it means what will be, will be. Honestly, Jamie, you worry too much. These things have a way of working themselves out. You'll see!"

"I hope you're right," I said, unconvinced.

"You must have spent the whole day with him," Andy said later that afternoon. "You were gone for hours."

It was a depressingly gray day, and a weak sun was trying to peep out from behind some low-lying clouds. We were walking briskly along the edge of the park, and I was trying to ignore the fact that my toes were nearly frozen in my socks and thin Italian sandals.

"Well, Mom thought it would be nice for Carlo to see New York City." Andy didn't answer and I stared at him. "We just did all the tourist stuff, Andy. It was nothing special."

Nothing special? Saturday in New York with Carlo *had* been special, I thought guiltily. In fact, it had been one of the most wonderful days I had ever spent.

"I see you did some shopping," Andy said, pointing to my new tan sandals.

"We saw these in an Italian leather shop down in the Village, and, well, Carlo wanted to buy them for me," I explained.

Andy took another look and frowned. "Not very practical, are they?"

"Maybe not for this weather," I admitted. I linked my arm through his, and tried for a light touch. "But if you and I were strolling around Rome right now, they'd be perfect."

"Stroll around Rome? What would I want to do a thing like that for?" Andy asked grumpily.

I stared at him in surprise. "Wouldn't you like to go there someday? Rome's supposed to be one of the most exciting cities in the world."

Andy turned up the collar on his red

windbreaker and said flatly, "No, I can't say that I would. There's plenty of places in *this* country I haven't even seen yet."

I sighed. When Andy gets in one of his moods, nothing suits him. The sun vanished behind the clouds then, and the flat November sky suddenly looked ominous.

"Looks like it may rain," he muttered. "We'd better head back."

"I've got an idea," I said brightly. "Why don't I call up Erin and Jeff? We can invite them over to play Trivial Pursuit with us this evening." I knew I couldn't face being alone with Andy. Anything to postpone the inevitable.

"If you want to," he said without enthusiasm.

"It'll be fun," I promised. If a miracle happens, I said silently. I sneaked a look at Andy's face and came to a glum conclusion: It was going to be a very long night.

"Oh, I know you'll get this one, Jeff!" Erin insisted an hour later. "What's the highest hand in straight poker?" She turned and grinned at Carlo. "Jeff's a real card freak."

Carlo smiled dutifully as Jeff smacked his fist triumphantly into his palm. "A royal flush. Way to go!"

It was cozy in the den. Carlo had helped me light a fire and the five of us were sprawled on cushions around the big oak coffee table. Andy had looked depressed when Carlo had wandered into the den and Erin had asked him to join us.

"No, that's okay," Carlo had said hesitantly. "You've got everything set up."

"Don't be silly. It's no trouble to add another player. C'mon and sit down." Erin had patted a cushion next to her, and the next thing you know, Carlo was in the game.

The first question he got was just sheer good luck. "Where's the Trevi Fountain?" I giggled.

"Rome," he deadpanned. "Was that a trick question?"

"Nope. You're just lucky," I told him. "But don't expect your luck to hold. There are some tough questions in here."

"I'll try to keep up with the rest of you," he promised.

Carlo did more than keep up. He took the lead immediately.

"I can't believe you're getting all the European questions," Erin told him. "Listen to this one. What German city do Italians call The Monaco of Bavaria?"

"That's easy," he said. "Munich."

"And I suppose you know the capital of

East Germany," Andy asked him coolly a few minutes later.

"Of course," Carlo answered in a frosty voice. "Berlin."

He finally lost a question on astronauts. "Who was the first man to hit a golf ball on the moon?" Jeff asked.

"Neil Armstrong," Carlo said confidently. Andy smugly gave the correct answer: Alan Shepard.

Around six-thirty, Mom and I put out her favorite dinner: do-it-yourself shish kebab. "It seems a shame to let that fire go to waste," she said. We moved the game board to the floor, and covered the coffee table with dishes of raw steak cubes, cherry tomatoes, and tiny onions. She added a giant casserole dish of fried rice, and passed out these lethal-looking skewers.

Everybody was quiet for a few minutes, threading the skewers with meat and vegetables.

"I feel like a Camp Fire girl," Erin kidded, holding the skewer over the roaring fire. "Have you ever gone camping, Carlo?" She swung around to face him.

"Many times." He squatted close to the fire, and expertly turned the skewer in one hand. "My family has a summer place in Trieste, and sometimes my brothers and I would sleep on the beach." He smiled at me.

"We cook meat over an open fire just like this."

"Trieste?" Jeff asked with interest. "Is that in Italy?"

"Yes, of course," Carlo said, surprised. "It's in the north, on the Adriatic Sea. It's near many famous beaches in Yugoslavia."

"Yugoslavia!" Jeff hooted. "People go swimming in Yugoslavia?"

"It's a famous resort area," Carlo said a little stiffly.

"Well, excu-u-u-se me!" Jeff teased. "I didn't even know it was on the ocean. It just doesn't sound like a hot vacation spot," he insisted. "I'll bet it can't beat Jones Beach, right, Erin?"

Erin thoughtfully bit into a roasted cherry tomato and shrugged. "I don't know. We could take Carlo there this summer and see what he thinks." She stopped and stared at Carlo. "What a dummy I am! You won't even be here next summer, will you?"

Carlo shook his head. "I'm afraid not," he said, looking right at me. He glanced at his calendar watch. "My time here is almost up. I'll be going home in December. Before Christmas."

Before Christmas! I couldn't believe it. But he was right, of course. I tuned out the rest of the conversation, trying to make sense out of the thoughts that were buzzing around in my head.

I sneaked a look at Carlo. His face was so serious as he dipped the skewer lightly into the flames. I couldn't take my eyes off his hands. They were the hands of an artist, I thought. I remembered the graceful way his fingers had raced over the organ at Pulsations, and the synthesizer at Macy's.

"Is anything wrong, Jamie?" Andy said quietly. "Or do you always cremate your food?"

"Cremate my — oh my gosh!" I yanked the skewer out of the fire and dumped it on my plate. The meat looked like lumps of charcoal.

"She likes it well-done," Erin teased.

"Or she's got a new recipe for Carbon 12," Andy piped up.

I joined in the laughter then, but I felt an enormous lump form in the back of my throat. *Before Christmas.* My eyes misted over, and my hand shook a little when I reached for the salad. *Before Christmas....*

I finally faced the truth: I didn't want Carlo to leave.

Not before Christmas. Not ever.

"I was right, wasn't I?" Andy said when everyone had left. We were standing in the kitchen, sipping hot chocolate, trying to avoid each other's eyes. Carlo had gone to bed, and the house was very still.

"What do you mean?" I stammered. I drained my cup and stared sightlessly out the kitchen window.

"I was right about Carlo." He paused. "And you."

"Andy. . . ." I tried to find the right words, but my mind was a blank.

"You care about him, don't you?" he went on in a flat voice. "You don't have to try to spare my feelings and deny it. I saw the way you looked at him tonight — and I saw the expression on your face when he talked about leaving." Andy started buttoning up his jacket, and I had a sudden impulse to put my arms around him, to ask him to stay.

"You know me too well," I muttered. "I always said you could read me like a book." I tried a laugh that didn't quite make it. "I didn't mean for it to happen," I said softly.

He gave a heavy sigh, and for a long moment, neither one of us said anything. "I know. I've been so busy lately, I haven't been able to spend much time with you. Maybe it was bound to happen."

Andy looked so tired and defeated that my heart went out to him. He wound a navy-blue muffler around his neck — the

one I had knitted for him last Christmas —
and picked up his car keys.

"It wasn't your fault," I said quickly.
"It's just — " I stopped. How could I explain Carlo?

"It's just that you've got a thing for
good-looking Italians," he said wryly. I
started to protest, but he cut me off. "Hey,
it's okay," he said, holding up his hand.
"I'm not going to jump off a bridge, you
know."

"I can't explain what happened," I said,
feeling miserable. "I don't really know,
myself."

"You don't have to explain it, Jamie,"
he said, looking at me with those deep
brown eyes. "For the past couple of weeks,
I've had this funny feeling that something
was wrong between us. I figured it was
Carlo, but I think I needed to hear it
straight from you." He touched my arm,
and then let his hand drop to his side. "I
think it's better that everything's finally
out in the open, don't you?"

Echoes of Erin. "Yes, I do," I said
weakly.

He stared at me and then said hesitantly,
"I guess you two are going to be spending
a lot of time together. I mean, like dating,
not just as friends."

"I haven't thought about it." I could

feel a hard knot forming in my chest. This was a million times harder than I had ever thought it would be.

"Well . . ." he said abruptly. He headed for the hall, and I followed him.

"Andy, wait. We can still be friends, can't we?"

"Sure, we can still be friends," he said quietly. When he opened the front door, a gust of frigid air enveloped us. "I'll always care about you, Jamie." He stood on the top step and ducked his head against the biting wind. Then he delivered the clincher. "But I don't think I want to see you for a while."

He said it so softly, it took a few seconds to sink in. "All right," I answered, fighting a lump in my throat as I tried to continue. "Whatever you want, Andy."

Mom took one look at my face early the next morning, and knew that something momentous had happened. She always gets up hours before anyone else, and she was alone in the kitchen when I wandered out at six o'clock.

"Too bad you missed the sunrise," she teased me. "If you'd been up just half an hour earlier. . . ." Then she put down her cup and stared at me. "Honey, what is it? You're not sick, are you?"

I dropped into a chair, and put my head in my hands. "I broke up with Andy," I said in a muffled voice. "Last night."

"Oh, Jamie, I'm sorry. Did you two have a fight?" She poured a cup of tea, and pushed it across the table to me.

"It's more complicated than that." I pulled my flannel robe tightly around me and held the steaming cup in my hands.

"Did he say something that upset you?" Her tone was gentle, concerned. Mom likes Andy, and acts like he's practically part of the family.

I paused, wondering how I could ever explain it to her. I couldn't even figure it out myself.

"No," I said finally. "We broke up because of Carlo."

"Carlo?"

I nodded. "Andy sensed that I really liked Carlo, and, well, I admitted that he was right."

"You and Carlo?" she said incredulously. "When did all this happen?"

"I guess it's been going on for a few weeks, but I didn't realize it until yesterday." I was glad that she only seemed surprised, not disapproving.

"This is kind of a shock," she admitted, carrying her dishes to the sink. "I was just saying to your father last night that you two seemed to be getting along a lot better, but I certainly didn't expect this." She paused and looked serious. "How did Andy take it?"

I answered her question indirectly. "Mom, I feel so confused, so — "

I never got to finish the sentence then, because Carlo wandered into the kitchen, smiling from ear to ear. He was dressed in a black turtleneck with tan cords and looked sensational. *"Buon giorno!"* he said enthusiastically. "A wonderful day, no?"

I looked at Carlo, and realized all over again what a terrific person he was. So warm, so special. Always so much fun, so full of life.

I pushed my regrets over Andy to the back of my mind, and grinned at Carlo. "A wonderful day, yes!" I told him.

Chapter 12

Thanksgiving was a funny, mixed-up kind
of day. Mom had to spend all morning at
the gallery, getting ready for a weekend
show, and Dad and Michael volunteered to
help her move some heavy metal sculptures
around the floor. I knew they'd be gone for
hours. I had seen the artist's last show, and
most of his pieces looked like they'd fallen
off the tail end of a Boeing 747.

That left Carlo and me alone with a
twenty-five pound turkey.

"Why did she buy such a big one?" Carlo
asked, panting slightly as he heaved the
bird into a roasting pan. It was eleven
o'clock, and we had just finished a late
breakfast before tackling the cooking.

"I don't know. Mom does the same thing
every year. And she insists on having the
works with it — everything from cranberry sauce to candied yams." I caught a

glimpse of myself in the kitchen mirror and tucked a stray lock of hair back into my barrette. I had dressed hurriedly in jeans and a sweat shirt that morning, and my bare feet were freezing on the kitchen floor. "Dad says she goes on a Norman Rockwell kick every Thanksgiving."

"Norman Rockwell?"

I paused, thinking. How to explain Norman Rockwell? "He painted a lot of very traditional American scenes," I said finally. "Families, holidays, that kind of thing."

"Ah."

"Mom comes from a big family, and — " I broke off suddenly, when I realized Carlo was standing right behind me. "Carlo, are you listening to me?"

"Always, *cara*. I am — how you say? Hanging on your every word." He wrapped his arms around my waist.

I laughed and moved away. "No time," I said in answer to his quick frown. "We have to start on the list." I held up a piece of notebook paper covered in Mom's neat handwriting.

"What list?" he asked disappointedly, making a move to put his arms around me again.

"The list of all the things we have to make for dinner," I said quickly. "The menu." I knew I had to get the words out fast. It was hard to think with Carlo's dark eyes staring so intently at me.

He reached over and kissed me playfully on the cheek.

"But the turkey will cook itself." He pointed to the microwave. "You explained it all to me before, with the magic rays."

I tried not to smile. "Yes, but there are tons of other things, Carlo. Chopping up the berries and shredding the orange peel for the cranberry relish alone will take at least an hour. You have to do it by hand, because the blender turns it to mush."

He took the list away from me, grasping me firmly with one arm. "We can go through this very quickly if we work on it together." He pointed to a word and frowned. "Tell me, what is yams?"

"Candied yams. I told you before, Carlo. That's something we make every year," I said, pointing to a bag of sweet potatoes on the counter. "You have to bake them in their jackets, and then peel them and add marshmallows and nuts and honey and — "

"All right," he said softly. "We will make the candied yams, if it will make you happy, *cara*."

"And cranberry sauce with shredded orange peel."

"Yes, the cranberry sauce with the

shredded orange peel." Carlo raised his head and gave a long-suffering sigh.

I consulted the list. "And icebox rolls and chestnut dressing."

"Icebox rolls and chestnut dressing." Carlo drew back slightly, and rolled his eyes to the ceiling.

"And two kinds of pie, pumpkin and apple crumb —"

Carlo groaned and released me. "Enough! You have convinced me. We will make every single thing on this list, even if it takes ten hours." He resolutely picked up a kitchen towel and wrapped it around his waist like an apron. "See, I am going to work. Now are you happy?"

The towel was a souvenir from Florida and it was emblazoned with palm trees and pink flamingos. Carlo looked so funny in it that I burst out laughing. He gave me an indignant look, and I reached over and squeezed his arm.

"Yes, I'm happy," I said, looking straight into his dark eyes. It was true. I was happier than I had ever been in my whole life.

"My compliments to the chefs," Dad said, raising a glass of apple cider in a toast. "I never would have believed you two could put together a meal like this."

All five of us had just sat down at the

dining room table. I had put out some hand-painted china that Mom saves for special occasions, and the table looked beautiful in the flickering candlelight.

Every Thanksgiving, we have a special tradition in our house. While Dad carves the turkey, everyone at the table mentions one thing that they're really thankful for. As usual, Michael refused to be serious, and said he was thankful for passing college calculus.

When it was Mom's turn, she bowed her head and said she was thankful that we had found a special friend who had made our lives so much brighter. When she looked up, she was staring right at Carlo. Dad reached over and clapped Carlo on the shoulder. "We're glad to have you with us, son."

I murmured something along the same lines, not daring to look at Carlo. Suddenly, Carlo cleared his throat and said formally, "I am thankful for my American family who has done so much for me — " he paused, and looked at me " — and I am thankful for Jamie." He said the last few words so softly, I didn't know if anyone else heard them. Just as I looked up, he said in a stronger voice, "She has given me much more than I could ever give to her."

*   *   *

I was so embarrassed, I took a giant
swig of cider and Michael had to thump
me on the back to stop me from choking.
Everyone laughed then, in a good-natured
way, and started passing platters of food
around. I sneaked a look at Carlo, secretly
pleased by what he had said about me.

The next couple of weeks passed in a
blur of fun and excitement. I was deliriously happy being with Carlo, and the two
of us spent practically every waking moment together. But the excitement was
mixed with sadness and I thought of the
opening line of a book we studied in English: "It was the best of times, it was the
worst of times."

The best part was that Carlo and I were
so happy together. The worst part was that
our time together was limited, and a lot of
the things we did had a last-time feeling to
them.

We were ice-skating at Ritter's Pond on
a Saturday morning in early December
when I suddenly felt my eyes misting over,
just thinking about saying good-bye to
Carlo. I was bending over to tie my skates,
fiddling with the laces, when the realiza-
tion hit. In just a few more weeks, he'd be
gone.

141

"Is everything okay, Jamie?" he asked, his voice heavy with concern. "Your eyes are red."

"Everything's fine," I assured him. "It's just the wind — it stings my eyelids." It was a raw day, and the pond was crowded with skaters. Carlo was having the time of his life doing figure eights, and skating a crazy dance to the rock music that was piped over the loudspeakers. He was dressed in a black pea coat and a bright red muffler, and I knew the image would stay in my mind forever.

"This is something we don't see much in Italy," he said, as we almost sideswiped a slow-moving couple in front of us.

"You don't have ice-skating?" I clung to his arm, even though I didn't need to, enjoying the feeling of closeness.

"Just indoor rinks. Not like this," he said, taking a deep breath of the biting air. "Ah," he said appreciatively. "Invigorating."

I smiled. Carlo had bought himself one of those increase-your-vocabulary books, and invigorating was on this week's word list. "Well, it's nice to know that you'll miss something about the States," I teased him. "Sometimes I think that you're dying to get back to Italy, back to civilization."

"There are many things I'll miss when

I go home, Jamie." He paused and bent his lips close to my cheek. "I will miss you most of all."

We skated silently for a few minutes then, while I bit my lip and made a furious effort not to cry. I was really annoyed with myself, and wished I could have more control over my emotions. The thing to do, I told myself, was to think positively. Think positively, and enjoy the time you have with him.

Half an hour later, Carlo was holding my hands, skating backward, when I recognized a familiar navy blue muffler flying in the wind in front of us. I craned my head to get a better look at the wearer, who was weaving in and out of the crowd, and spotted Andy. Andy! I opened my mouth to call his name, but the sound died in my throat. What was I thinking of? I had broken up with him.

"Tell me if I'm going to run into something," Carlo pleaded, his skates kicking up little icy pebbles. Carlo was a skillful, if reckless skater, and we rounded a turn at breakneck speed.

"I'll tell you," I said, my thoughts still on the boy in the navy blue muffler. The muffler I had knitted for him just last winter, I reminded myself. So much had changed since then!

Only Carlo would decide to go out for ice cream in sub-zero weather. I was still half frozen from skating, when he said excitedly, "Look, there's a Baskin Robbins. Maybe they have Pumpkin Delight." He pointed to a small ice-cream parlor at the edge of the park.

"You really feel like ice cream on a day like this?" I asked incredulously.

"Of course," he said with that lazy smile that made my heart turn over. "Italians are brought up on *gelato*, don't you know that?"

"I'll take your word for it," I said through my chattering teeth.

A few minutes later, we were seated at a back booth in a cheerful little place full of skaters. Carlo looked around, delighted.

"See, what did I tell you? Everyone had the same idea." He always liked being in crowds. "And I see they have some new flavors," he said approvingly. "The Banana Supreme should be good . . . but look, they no longer have Bubble Gum."

"Maybe it wasn't a big seller," I said, nearly numb from the cold.

"What would you like? You really should try the Choco-Peanut Butter," he said helpfully.

Just thinking about ice cream gave me

a toothache. "Carlo, I don't want any ice cream," I said as gently as I could. "Just get me something to drink, please."

"Hot chocolate," he said, snapping his fingers. "Exactly what you need. That will warm you up in a minute."

"Carlo, they probably don't have hot chocolate," I called after him, but it was too late. He vanished into a crowd around the counter.

I had just settled back in the booth, rubbing my sore ankles, when Erin saw me and cried happily, "Jamie! I haven't seen you in ages!" She stared at the black pea coat that Carlo had thrown over the seat. "Who are you with?" she asked, flopping down across from me.

"Carlo," I told her.

"Ah-ha! I should have guessed." She leaned forward and stared at me. "You look cold, but happy."

I laughed. "You're right on both counts. We've been skating all afternoon, and I think I've got frostbite." I gently flexed my sore fingers, wondering if I'd ever be able to use them again.

"He's here, you know," Erin said, lowering her voice. She glanced around the crowded room like a spy.

"Who?"

She rolled her eyes, and leaned even

closer. "Who do you think? Andy!" she whispered. "He's been skating for hours."

I nodded. "I know. I saw him just for a second, but he didn't see me."

She waited a minute, and then said, "He still cares about you, you know."

I licked my lips a little nervously, wishing Carlo would get back with his Papaya Fling, or whatever he was ordering. "That's over," I said simply.

"Not for him, it's not. He asks about you all the time." She nodded very seriously. "He's taking Sherry out, but it doesn't mean anything."

"Oh." I felt like someone had dropped a stone in my stomach.

"You knew that, didn't you?" she asked, reading my expression.

"Oh, of course." I laughed, and scanned the crowd for Carlo.

"Well, you can't expect him to sit home every night," she said reasonably, "and after all, you have Carlo."

"That's right." I tried to put an agreeable look on my face. "I'm just a little surprised, that's all. I didn't think Sherry was his type." I thought I was his type, I added silently.

Erin put her hand over her mouth, in case anyone in Baskin Robbins could read lips. She was just winding up to give me her opinion of Sherry, when Carlo reappeared, holding a double-fudge sundae, and a strange concoction in a steaming metal glass.

"What's that?" I asked, as Erin scooted over to make room for him.

"Your hot chocolate," he said, putting it in front of me with a flourish. "If you know how to ask, nothing is impossible. All it takes is Italian know-how."

"But they don't have hot chocolate here," Erin objected. "I asked for some."

Carlo gave a self-satisfied smile. "That is correct. They do not have hot chocolate."

"Then what's this?" I took a tentative sip. It tasted odd, yet familiar.

Carlo shrugged. "A malted milk. A *heated* malted milk." When we stared at him in amazement, he laughed and snapped his fingers. "What did I tell you. Italian know-how!"

Chapter 13

"We're supposed to get a lot more snow today," Mom said a few days later at breakfast. She pulled back the kitchen window curtain and peered out at the swirling flakes that had already blanketed the backyard. "They're talking about another five or six inches, so be sure you bundle up. And call me if there's any trouble with the school bus. I'll zip home and pick you up."

"Will do," I said, munching on a croissant. I sneaked a look at Carlo, who was staring out the window, fascinated.

"Beautiful," he said softly. "Look, Jamie, have you ever seen such a sight?"

"Very nice," I said politely. I was much more interested in looking at Carlo than at the backyard. In fact, I could hardly take my eyes off him. He was wearing a white fisherman's knit sweater with jeans and boots, and looked like an Italian movie star.

"Very nice? Is that all you can say?" He looked wounded. "It's more than very nice . . . it's *magnifico*!" I smiled. Even though Carlo's English was just about perfect, he still used Italian when he was excited. He spread his hands expressively, and breathed a sigh. "Look at the way the snow covers the bushes. They look like ice sculptures. And the sky. What a sky! See, it's gray over there, by the horizon, but in the center, it's shiny and pink, almost like a pearl." He tugged at my sleeve, almost sloshing my hot chocolate. "Haven't you ever noticed that before?" he demanded.

"No, I guess I haven't," I answered, laughing. It always amazed me that Carlo could get so passionately interested in things. A sky, a painting, or a piece of music could capture his attention for hours. "To me, it's just a November sky."

"December," my mother corrected, pouring herself a cup of coffee. "I hate to say it, but it's the first of the month today." She smiled at Carlo. "December is absolutely our worst month at the gallery. We stay open late every single night, and my boss panics if the inventory isn't done by New Year's Day. You know, it makes me tired just to think about it."

I stared at the kitchen calendar, tuning

out the rest of her conversation. There it was in black and white: December first. It took me a few seconds to absorb it. This was the first, and Carlo was leaving on the fifteenth, so . . . I jumped up, banging my shin on the table.

"Jamie," my mother said reproachfully. She reached for a roll of paper towels and began mopping up her spilled coffee.

"Sorry," I said quickly. "I just remembered I've got to hunt for my math book." I left the kitchen at a half run, and didn't slow down until I got to my room and safely closed the door behind me. Fourteen days. Just thinking about it made my eyes start to water. My chest felt so tight I could hardly breathe. I was standing in front of the mirror, trying to pull myself together, when Mom tapped on the door. "Honey, did you hear the radio report? They just announced school's out today because of the weather."

"Okay, thanks," I said. I had to force the words past a giant lump in my throat, and my voice sounded muffled.

The door opened softly. "Are you okay?" Mom said in a low voice. "You look white as a sheet."

"I'm okay," I muttered.

"You're not sick, are you?" She put her hand on my forehead, just like she used to do when I was a little kid. I shook my head, wordlessly, and she understood. "Oh, honey," she said sympathetically, taking my hands in hers. "You're not sick, but you're upset, aren't you?" She glanced at the open door and lowered her voice. "It's Carlo, isn't it?"

"Yes," I muttered. I could feel some tears lurking behind my eyelids, so I ran a brush through my hair, reminding myself how awful I look when I cry. Some girls look sort of tragic and interesting, but my nose always runs and my eyes get puffy. Not a pretty sight.

My mother leaned her head against mine and gave a wistful smile. "You always knew he'd have to leave, Jamie," she said gently.

"I know, but I didn't think I'd feel this way. Especially not in the beginning." I had to smile, thinking of my first impression of Carlo.

"In the beginning, you said four months would seem like forever," she reminded me.

"I know, but I was wrong. The time flew by."

"And your feelings changed," she added thoughtfully. My room was so quiet you could hear a pin drop, and my mother sighed and walked over to the window. "You have fourteen days left with him," she said quietly. "Do you want to throw them away?"

"Throw them away?" I asked, startled. "Is that what you think I'm doing?"

"You will if you fall apart every time you think about him leaving," she said pointedly. She turned to face me, and her deep eyes were warm with sympathy. "Look, Jamie, I know you're feeling down right now, but did it ever occur to you that maybe this is a rough time for Carlo, too? He's been away from his family for months, and now he's facing the loss of someone he's gotten very attached to. Part of him wants to go home to Italy, and part of him wants to stay here with us. It can't be easy for him."

She was right, of course. If I hadn't been so wrapped up in my own feelings, I would have seen it myself. "Do you really think that he's gotten that attached to me?" I asked hesitantly.

She smiled at me. "I know he has." She glanced at her watch and gave me a swift hug. "I've got to run now, honey. Are you feeling better?" She pulled back to look at me.

"Much better."

"And you're not going to spend the day moping around?"

"Are you kidding?" I pretended to be indignant. "When Carlo only has two weeks left in the United States? I've got a million things to do, a million places to take him. I don't have a minute to waste!"

"Well, I'm glad to hear it," she said, laughing. "What are your plans for today?"

I looked at the swirling snow and got a sudden inspiration. "Today we're going to do something I bet Carlo's never done before," I said mischievously.

"Really?" She arched an eyebrow inquisitively.

"I bet he's never done this," I chuckled, "because Rome hardly ever gets any snow."

"You're going ice-skating again?" she asked dubiously.

"Better than that. We're going sledding!"

"I can't imagine how little kids do this," Carlo said grumpily a couple of hours later. He had just fallen off the sled for the third time, and his designer jeans were soaking wet.

"It's easier when you're a little kid," I told him. "For one thing, you can squeeze your body onto a three-foot sled." I rolled off my battered wooden sled, and grabbed the tow rope, ready to drag it up the hill once more. Carlo grabbed my ankle playfully, almost pulling me down beside him.

"Have mercy," he pleaded. "I'm getting snowbite."

"Frostbite," I corrected automatically. "And if you had borrowed those waterproof ski pants of Michael's, you wouldn't be so wet." I looked at him lying miserably in the snow, and couldn't resist a final shot. "And anyway, it's all your own fault. Nobody wears his best jeans to go sledding."

"I do," Carlo said firmly. He looked disdainfully at the rest of the kids sledding down Tower Hill. "No style at all," he sighed. Carlo had turned down my offer of an Army parka and had insisted on wearing a black turtleneck ski sweater with a salmon-colored muffler. If you could overlook the fact that his nose was red and his teeth were chattering, he looked terrific.

I laughed and started up the hill when he suddenly scrambled to his feet and threw an arm over my shoulder. "How long have we been out here?" he asked plaintively.

"I don't know, about an hour and a half, I guess. Why?"

"An hour and a half?" He groaned theatrically. "You know that famous American saying, 'time flies when you're having fun'?" He tugged vigorously on his sled and fell into place beside me.

"Of course I know it. It's one of the first

American phrases you learned."

"Well, it's a lie," he said teasingly. "In fact —"

I never knew what Carlo was going to say next because he was interrupted by a shrill shout from behind us.

"Hi, guys! Isn't this great? I haven't done this since I was eight years old."

It was Sherry, smiling from ear to ear, and talking a mile a minute. I smiled and waved automatically as she approached us, but I wasn't really listening to Sherry at all. I was staring at the boy next to her. It was Andy.

"Hello, Jamie." He paused and nodded curtly to Carlo. "Carlo." Then he stared at me, and I had absolutely no idea what was going through his mind.

There was a long silence, and just when I thought I'd go crazy if somebody didn't say something, Carlo jumped in. "It looks like everybody got the same idea."

Sherry nodded enthusiastically. "It seemed like the perfect way to spend the day, but I had no idea it would be so cold." She shivered, stamped her feet prettily like a race horse, and pretended to pout. She was wearing black bib ski overalls with a powder blue jacket and looked terrific. A crazy thought popped into my head: Blue is Andy's favorite color. "We're just about ready to call it quits. Want to get some lunch with us?"

"We'd love to," Carlo answered, just as I said, "We can't."

Carlo and I looked at each other in surprise, while Sherry giggled. "Well, which is it?" she asked. She gave Andy a mischievous little smile and he looked uncomfortable. "Either you can or you can't. Unless somebody isn't telling the truth," she went on in a singsong voice. She linked her arm through Andy's in a really possessive way, and I could feel my temper flaring.

"We're *both* telling the truth," I said sweetly. "You see, the truth is, we'd love to have lunch with you, but unfortunately, we can't."

"We can't?" Carlo asked, surprised.

"That's right," I said, wishing I could give him a swift kick in the shins. "I promised Mom I'd fix dinner for her tonight."

"But it's only twelve o'clock. You've got hours yet." Sherry wasn't going to let me off the hook that easily.

"We've having a roast. It takes hours to cook," I said hurriedly, grabbing Carlo's arm and pulling him away. "Have fun," I said cheerfully. Seeing Andy had shaken me up more than I had expected, but there was no reason to let Sherry in on the secret.

"Oh," Sherry said, sounding disappointed. "We'll see you guys tomorrow at school, then."

"That's right. See you then!" I gave a bright smile, like I was having the time of my life. I could feel Andy's eyes boring holes in me, but I refused to look at him again, and started walking away very quickly.

"Why didn't you want to see Sherry and Andy?" Carlo said later that afternoon. "You used to be good friends." We were sitting side by side at the kitchen table with grilled cheese sandwiches and mugs of tomato soup.

I didn't want to admit that it made me uncomfortable to see Andy with another girl. "I'd rather spend my time with you," I said simply. I put the kettle on for tea and glanced outside at the darkening sky before I sat back down next to Carlo. The kitchen was warm and cozy, and it was nice to feel isolated from the rest of the world.

"Jamie, I don't want you to lose your friends because of me," Carlo began.

"Let's not waste time talking about other people," I said softly. I looked across the table at him, and tried to ignore the countdown that was still running in my mind. Fourteen days. Fourteen days.

"What would you like to talk about,

cara?" He smiled and held my hand.

I didn't even have to think about that one. "You, of course."

He smiled and leaned back in his chair. "But you already know everything about me. My life is" — he struggled with an idiom — "an open book."

"No, it isn't," I insisted, pouring out two cups of steaming tea. "I know you live in Rome, and have a summer place in the country. . . ."

"Very good," he teased me.

"And you have two sisters, fourteen cousins, three dogs, and four cats."

"My favorite color is red," he prompted me. "Just in case you're interested."

"I already knew that." I paused, tracing a design on the tablecloth with the end of my spoon. "There's one thing you've never mentioned."

He took a swig of tea and added a heaping spoonful of honey. "And that is?"

I took a deep breath. "You've never told me if you have a girl friend back in Rome."

He put his cup down very carefully and looked very seriously at me. "Is that important?"

"Yes," I told him. "It's important for me to know." I waited, and when he didn't say anything I went on. "You see, you know everything about me. You know what I look like when I wake up in the morning, and that I love English and hate math. And you've met all my friends. Even Andy."

He smiled then, and I think he understood. "If you're asking, is there one special girl waiting for me back in Rome, the answer is no." He edged a little closer and put his arm around me. "I've dated a few girls, Jamie. Each one had something that appealed to me. One was pretty, one could make me laugh, one was very intelligent."

"Sounds like you had more than one girl friend," I muttered. I was beginning to wish I hadn't started this conversation.

"You could say that." He nodded. "But that was because I never expected to find everything I wanted in *one* person." His dark eyes were shining, and he gently touched my cheek. "I didn't think anyone like you existed." He put his arm around me, and for a long moment we hugged each other. Finally, he drew back and said, "You know what I think?"

"What?" I asked in a daze.

"I think we'd better eat our tomato soup before it gets cold." He winked at me then, and calmly reached for a cracker. "Eat up!" he urged, placing a spoon in my hand. "You're going to need all the energy you can get."

"I am?"

"You are," he said firmly. "Because after lunch, I, Carlo Santini, am going to challenge you to a snowball fight!"

As usual, Carlo had managed to amaze me again.

"You will come to the party, won't you?" Erin asked a few days later. "I'm having twenty-four kids. It should really be a blast."

"What's the date again?" I hedged.

"Jamie! Honestly, you've got a mind like a sieve. It's Friday, December fourteenth. Look I'll write it on your notebook, if you want." We were standing in the hall between classes, and I backed against the wall as Erin waved a magic marker at me.

"That's okay, I'll remember," I told her.

"Yes, but will you come?" She gave me an exasperated look. "Everyone is going to be there, and my mother's letting me order pizza from Pappy's." Suddenly she stopped and said sympathetically, "It's Carlo, isn't it? Will he still be here?"

"He's leaving the next day," I said quietly. "Flight six-oh-four from Kennedy at eleven-thirty." I had said the numbers so often to myself, I knew them by heart.

"Gee," Erin said, "that's tough. I knew he was leaving around Christmas, but I guess I thought he'd be here a little longer."

I shrugged. "He wants to spend the holidays with his family, so he's leaving as soon as we start our winter vacation." It was all perfectly logical when I explained it that way. The only thing that didn't make sense was why I felt so awful just thinking about it.

Erin paused and took a quick look up and down the hall. "I'm having Sherry, and she's going to ask Andy. Will that bother you?"

"Bother me? Of course not," I said, forcing a smile. "We're still friends, you know. It's not as if we hate each other."

"No, of course not," Erin said quickly. "I just didn't want to make things hard for you, that's all." She shifted her books to one arm and ran a hand through her sleek, dark hair. "Look, I didn't realize that it would be Carlo's last night here, so if you guys want to skip the party, I understand. Maybe you want to be alone."

I thought for a moment. I wanted Carlo to have a special night to remember — a night filled with fun and excitement. It would be better to be surrounded by people that last night.

"No, I'd like to go to the party with him, Erin." I smiled at her. "You can count on us."

Chapter 14

Erin's pine-paneled basement was so jammed with kids you could hardly breathe, but as far as I was concerned, Carlo and I could have been alone on a desert island. I had my arms around his neck as we swayed back and forth to an old Beach Boys song.

"I always think of this as American music," Carlo said, straining to catch the lyrics that hung like threads in the air. He sighed and looked around approvingly. "American music, American parties, American girls."

"So that's all I am to you," I said, pretending to sulk. "An American girl?"

He laughed, a deep sound that made my breath catch in my throat. "No, *cara*," he said softly. "You're much more than that."

"Hey, you two." Sherry's high-pitched voice cut through Brian Wilson's steady drumbeat. "You're not going to keep Carlo all to yourself on his last night here, are you?"

"I certainly am," I said sweetly. I was just about to make an excuse to move away when Carlo stopped me.

"Where's Andy?" he asked, looking over Sherry's shoulder.

Sherry flushed, but she made a quick recovery and said gaily, "Oh, he had to work tonight. Something came up at Pappy's at the last minute." She caught me staring at her, and flashed a brittle smile. "You know what his boss is like — a real slave-driver."

I nodded, not believing a word of it. Had they had a fight? I wondered, as Carlo whisked me away for another dance. It was a fast one, and within seconds I was caught up in the pulsating rhythm of a Rolling Stones song.

The evening passed like a dream, and I tried to enjoy every minute, refusing to think of what the next day would bring. Around ten-thirty, we bumped into Erin and Jeff at the snack table, and they asked Carlo about his plans.

"So it's back to Rome tomorrow," Jeff said, clapping Carlo on the back. "Well, take care of yourself, man. This place sure won't be the same without you." His brown eyes were serious, and I knew that he really meant it. With his honesty and terrific sense of humor, Carlo had managed to win over most of the guys in the past few weeks.

"We're sure going to miss you," Erin piped up. "You'll have to let us know what you're doing. You and Jamie are going to stay in touch, aren't you?"

"Of course," I said quickly. I smiled and fought back a panicky feeling that threatened to rise to the surface. What if I never saw him again — never heard from him again!

"That's good," Erin said approvingly. "Because I want a full report on what the Italian kids are wearing this spring. They say that those big T-shirts are going to be popular, Jamie," Erin prattled on. "We'll have to get some and wear them with stirrup pants."

I smiled and nodded, as Carlo squeezed my hand. I didn't want to think about spring without Carlo! It felt terrific just standing next to him, and I wished the evening never had to end. We danced a dozen more dances, and at midnight Erin's mother flashed the lights twice, to a chorus of moans.

"That means the party's over," I explained to Carlo, who gave me a puzzled frown.

"Hey, do you guys want a ride?" Sherry called cheerfully from across the room. "Mike MacKenzie is giving me a lift."

I looked at Carlo and he shook his head. "I think we'll walk," he said, helping me with my coat. "If that's okay with Jamie," he added politely.

"That's fine with me," I told him. Erin's party had been fun, but I was suddenly eager to be someplace far away, alone with Carlo. There were a million things I wanted to say to him, things that would be impossible to put into a letter.

It was a raw, foggy night, and a piercing wind whipped around our ankles as we made our way home. A pale moon made a brief appearance and then vanished behind a heavy layer of clouds.

"Not very nice weather," I muttered, huddling against Carlo. "Especially for your last night here." I hoped I sounded a lot braver than I felt. Every time I thought of Carlo's plane leaving, I wanted to burst into tears.

There was a heavy silence, and then Carlo said quietly, "You don't know how much I'm going to miss you, *cara*." He was staring straight ahead, his expression serious. "But, there's no other way," he breathed softly. "I've gone over it a hundred times."

I bit my lip and wondered what to say. What did he mean, he'd gone over it? I thought about it for a minute, and then it dawned on me. Maybe he was actually considering staying in the States! My heart did a little flip-flop, and I nearly tripped. Maybe all he needed was a little encouragement.

Should I tell him how much he meant to me? I tucked my hand in his, and we walked silently for a couple of blocks.

Finally, I couldn't stand it any longer. "Carlo," I said hopefully, "is there any chance of your staying with us for another semester? I know my folks would be thrilled. And I would, too."

"Jamie," he said quietly, "you know I would if it were possible."

"But it *is* possible," I said quickly. "It wouldn't be any problem at all. Lots of exchange students stay for the whole year. In fact, Mom was just saying yesterday that she wished you could stay for the spring semester."

He laughed softly. "That's very nice of her, Jamie. But you know something?" He stopped under the glare of a yellow streetlight, and rested both hands on my shoulders. He looked very handsome in the strange half light, and I felt a familiar catch in my throat.

"What?" I asked, in a quavery voice.

"Jamie," he said, looking right at me with his piercing dark eyes, "my place is in Rome. Just as you belong here, in the States."

"But how can you say that?" I pleaded. I felt afraid and angry, at the same time. Afraid that I would never see Carlo again, angry that he could change everything with one word, and was stubbornly refusing to say it. "You belong in the States, too. You're practically an American now."

"Jamie —"

"No, listen to me. You've changed so much in the past few months, Carlo." I paused, trying to find the right words to convince him. "Didn't you notice the way everyone treated you like one of the gang tonight? You're not an outsider anymore. You're one of us."

A stabbing gust of wind grabbed me, and I shivered in my wool coat.

"Come," Carlo said gently, "you are cold. We must go home now."

"But I don't *want* to go home!" I said, my voice shaking. I could feel the tears spilling over my cheeks, and tried to will them away. "This is probably the last chance I'll ever get to talk to you alone," I said hoarsely. I was crying so hard, I could hardly get the words out. "Carlo, I don't want you to leave tomorrow."

"Oh, Jamie," he murmured, pulling me close to him. "I don't want to leave you, either. But, believe me, I must go." I buried my face against his coat, only half listening to what he was saying. "My family is in Rome, and my friends," he said, stroking my hair. "You know that."

"But you're part of my life here," I said stubbornly. "What will I do without you?"

"I have a life there, too, *cara*," he said gently. "And it's not the end, you know." He pulled back and raised my chin so that I had to look at him. "We will see each other again."

"We will?"

"Of course." He smiled and wiped my wet cheeks with his fingertips. "Maybe in the summer, or maybe during a vacation. I will come to you, or you will come to me."

"But in the meantime. . . ?"

"In the meantime. . . ." And then he kissed me. I put my arms around him and held him so tightly I could feel his heart beating. "Never forget me, *cara*," he murmured. The moon popped out from behind the clouds just then, and I knew that every detail — the yellow streetlamp, the snow-flakes nestling in Carlo's hair, the rough wool of his jacket — would be etched in my mind forever.

"I never will," I promised him.

He took me firmly by the hand then, and we headed for home.

It was impossible to sleep, and I felt more dead than alive when Mom tapped gently on my bedroom door the next morning and handed me a cup of tea.

"There's no time for breakfast, honey," she said. "I figured you'd rather have the extra few minutes of sleep."

"You're right," I said, glancing in the mirror. Why hadn't I done something with my hair? It was hanging limply about my shoulders, and I knew I didn't have time to fix it now.

"We're leaving in about twenty minutes," Mom said. "You know what that airport traffic is like."

I nodded, wriggling into a pair of jeans. "Is, uh, Carlo all packed?"

"Dad and Michael are loading up the car right now." She peered at my pale face and said slowly. "Honey, are you going to be okay? You don't look too great."

"Flattery will get you everywhere," I said, forcing a joke to reassure her. "I'm just a little tired, that's all."

"Well, maybe you can take a nap this afternoon," she said briskly, and headed for the door. "Michael's going out for the day, so the house will be quiet." She stopped, realizing what she had just said. "It will be too quiet," she said, turning to face me. We looked at each other for a moment, and the truth suddenly dawned on me: She's going to miss him, too. "I hate good-byes," she muttered then, and walked quickly out of the room.

I knew the scene at the airport wouldn't be easy. Luckily, it was short. The traffic was worse than Dad had expected, and by the time Carlo had checked his luggage, and had his passport stamped, they were already announcing his flight.

"Are you sure you've got everything?" Mom asked him for the dozenth time. "You've got money, and you've got something to read on the plane. . . ."

"Yes, I have money, I have magazines," he assured her.

"And your parents are going to meet you in Rome?" Dad questioned.

"My whole family is going to meet me in Rome," Carlo said with a grin. "Aunts, uncles, cousins, even the grandparents from the country. You don't know what a big deal this is to them." He looked at me and smiled. "They've practically declared a national holiday."

I tried to smile back, but my face felt frozen. I knew what he was trying to do — making silly jokes, trying to keep the mood light — and I was grateful for it. It couldn't erase the pain, though, or the sick, empty feeling I had in the pit of my stomach. Carlo, Carlo, I said silently. What am I going to do without you?

Before I knew it, we were at the gate, and Mom, Dad, and Michael each enveloped him in a bear hug. "Make sure you write to me in English," Michael teased him.

"I'll do better than that. I'll send you that Pelé sweat shirt you wanted."

Then everybody hugged him again, and Dad clapped him on the back and said how much all of us were going to miss him. I hung in the background, wanting to throw my arms around him, yet afraid to make a move. What if I made an idiot out of myself and broke down, right in the airport?

Mom must have sensed that I wanted to be alone with him, because she managed to steer Michael and Dad to the glass window that covered the far wall of the terminal. "Look, if we stand over here, we can watch Carlo's plane taking off," she said brightly.

They drifted off then, after another round of hugs, and finally Carlo and I were facing each other, standing just inches apart. He smiled that wonderful smile that always made me feel I was someone special.

I couldn't meet his eyes. "I hate good-byes," I muttered, staring at my shoes. The next thing I knew, Carlo had his arms around me, and I buried my face in his neck. Don't cry, don't cry, I said silently.

"I know, *cara*," he said in a sad voice. "I do, too. But you know something?" He drew back and looked at me very seriously. "You have to say good-bye before you can say hello again."

I tried to answer, but the words stuck in my throat. "Carlo —" I knew if I tried to talk, I'd burst out crying.

"Shhh," he said soothingly. "It's going to be all right, Jamie. We will see each other again. Never forget that." He stared at me for a long moment, while I tried to control the hot tears that were lurking behind my eyelids. I knew that in another five seconds, they'd be spilling down my cheeks.

"Good-bye, Jamie," he whispered. Then he kissed me lightly, turned, and walked quickly through the double glass doors toward the tarmac.

A little later, the plane lifted from the

ground, soared high above the runway, and turned eastward. I watched the plane grow smaller, a tiny flicker of silver against the pale blue of the morning sky. Finally it rose above the clouds and disappeared completely.

Carlo was gone.

"How'd it go?" Erin said softly that evening. "Was it really awful saying good-bye to him?"

"It was over so quickly," I told her. "One minute we were standing with our arms around each other, and the next minute, he was gone."

Erin shook her head sympathetically as we scooted into a back booth at Pappy's. "I hate good-byes," she said, tossing her red poncho over her head. She was wearing a black turtleneck sweater with a tan leather vest, and her dark hair was shining.

"You have to say good-bye before you can say hello again," I murmured, and she gave me a puzzled look.

"What did you say?"

"Nothing," I said shortly. "I was just remembering something Carlo told me."

It was crowded at Pappy's, and I sneaked a quick look toward the back of the room, half afraid that I might spot Andy working behind the counter. He's probably not even here, I thought, relieved. Nobody should have to work on Saturday nights, he used to tell me, his eyes serious. It's a night to spend with your girl. . . .

I ducked my head and pretended to be studying the menu, but Erin was too quick for me.

"He's not here," Erin said matter-of-factly, her eyes meeting mine over the top of the menu.

As usual our thoughts were in tune. "Since when have you become a psychic?" I muttered.

She smiled and closed the menu. "I'm not," she grinned. "Just a lucky guess." She waved to someone across the room and then looked at me very seriously. "Andy's still on your mind, isn't he?"

I shrugged. "Not really. I guess it's just that this place brings back some memories. After all, we went out together a long time." I paused. "How did you know he wouldn't be here tonight?"

Erin grinned. "A little bird told me. A bird with long brown hair."

Sherry.

She waited until the waitress took our order and said, "Would it bother you to see him again? With someone else, I mean?"

"No," I said too quickly, and she raised

her eyebrows. "I don't know," I said honestly. "All I can think of now is Carlo."

I glanced at my watch and sighed. *Carlo.* It was hard to believe that he would be landing in Rome in half an hour. And it seemed even more remarkable that just a few hours ago, he had kissed me right in the middle of JFK International Airport. He had looked so handsome, with his blazing black eyes and dazzling smile.

Erin's voice brought me back to the present. "Well, here's to whatever," she said, raising her glass in a mock salute.

I hadn't even noticed the icy glass of Coke in front of me. I picked it up in a trance, my fingers chilled, and clinked it against Erin's glass. "To Carlo," I said softly.

"To Carlo," she repeated solemnly. She stared at me for a moment and then said in a low voice, "It's going to be okay, Jamie, it really is."

I nodded, not trusting my voice. "Sure," I said finally, managing a tight smile. "It's just going to take a little time."

My mother said almost the exact same thing to me a couple of days later. We were finishing up the dinner dishes, and a Billy Joel song was humming softly on the kitchen radio. It was one of Carlo's favorites, and a bittersweet sadness welled up in me. Carlo, I said silently. I miss you.

"Give it a little time," my mother said gently, reading my expression.

I bit my lip and frowned. "Does it show much?"

She smiled and put her arm around me. "I'm afraid so. Remember that night at dinner when Carlo told you that you have 'mirror eyes'?"

I nodded. "Michael laughed so hard he nearly fell off the chair."

"Carlo was right," she went on. She smiled and ran her hand through my hair, the way she used to do when I was little. "All anyone has to do is look in your eyes, and all your thoughts and feelings are right there for them to see. You don't keep anything hidden."

"Maybe it would be better if I did," I said wryly.

"No, it's better to feel things, Jamie. Don't ever keep anything bottled up inside."

When the phone rang a few minutes later, I picked it up automatically, never guessing who was on the other end.

"*Cara.*" The voice was warm, wonderfully familiar, and seemed so close. The wall phone is beside the kitchen window, and I stared out at the inky darkness, willing myself to be calm.

"Carlo," I gulped, unable to focus my thoughts. My mind was racing. There were a million things I wanted to tell him, but the words wouldn't come out. "How are you?" I gasped.

He chuckled softly. "I'm fine. And you?" he added politely.

"I'm fine," I repeated like a robot. "Just fine." My hand gripped the receiver tightly. "It's almost Christmas, you know," I said stupidly. Of course he knows it's almost Christmas, you idiot. He's in Italy, not on Mars!

"Over here, too," he said, laughing. "I just wanted to see how you were, and I wanted to ask about your family."

"Oh, they're fine, too," I babbled on. "Mom is fine, and Dad is fine, and Michael. . . ." I was as breathless as if I had just run a marathon. "Michael is fine, too." Brilliant conversation, Jamie. Really brilliant. The most important call of your life, and you're rambling on like a six-year-old. I squeezed my eyes tightly shut and tried to concentrate on the voice on the other end of the wire.

I decided to start over. "I never expected you to call me," I said in a little voice.

There was a slight pause, and then Carlo's voice raced toward me once more, warm and reassuring. "I had to hear your voice again," he said simply. "Don't forget I've heard your voice every day for . . . what? Three months?"

"Three months, two weeks, and four days," I said promptly, and Carlo burst out laughing. "That is, if anyone's counting," I went on jokingly.

"It's nice to know that you care," Carlo said in a voice that was half teasing.

I care, I said silently. "Are you having a good time with your family?" I said, more relaxed now.

"It was a mob scene at the airport," Carlo laughed. "All the relatives from Naples and Trieste showed up — it was really a circus. And I'm seeing a lot of old friends. One of my cousins is throwing a welcome-home party for me tonight."

A picture of Carlo suddenly popped into my head. He was flashing that thousand-kilowatt smile and entertaining a group of friends. Music was playing somewhere and there was a beautiful girl next to him.

"And you?" he was saying, and I pulled my mind back out of the daydream.

"Oh, I'm busy," I said, forcing a laugh. "Lots of Christmas parties and dances." I bit my lip and wondered what to say next.

"I miss you, Jamie," he said in a very low voice.

I felt thrilled and excited inside. "I miss you, too," I whispered. "I've missed you every minute since you left."

"I'm glad."

Mom walked in the kitchen then, and gave me a curious glance. "I'll write to you tonight," I said suddenly. "Would you like that?"

"Very much, *cara*. Then I would know that I am still in your thoughts."

Carlo was never out of my thoughts, even in the middle of all the Christmas rush. I was sitting at the kitchen table, writing to him on pale blue airmail stationery, while Mom put the finishing touches on a gigantic turkey. It was late afternoon on Christmas Eve, and I thought of Carlo struggling to lift another turkey, back on Thanksgiving Day.

"What's so funny?" Mom said, smiling at me.

"Oh, I was just thinking of Carlo." I paused. "I wish he could have stayed with us for Christmas," I said wistfully.

"His family would have been disappointed," she said gently. "Although, I must admit, I would have enjoyed taking him to the tree-lighting ceremony tonight."

Every Christmas my whole family goes to City Square to watch the lights go on a thirty-foot tree. For the past two years, Andy has come with us, and it seemed a little funny to pile into the car without him later that evening.

"Look, Jamie, it's even more beautiful than last year," Mom said softly as we edged our way to the front of the crowd. She was right. The towering pine tree was ablaze with hundreds of cranberry-colored lights that burned like rubies against the dark night. We sang carols for a while, and then when Mom struck up a conversation with one of her friends, I wandered over to a concession stand to buy some hot cider.

It was exactly the kind of Christmas Eve I like, cold and crisp, and I stamped my boots softly against the packed snow as I stood in line. My hands were freezing so I plunged them in my pockets.

The line was moving steadily forward when I heard someone behind me say, "I bet you forgot your gloves again."

Andy. "How did you know?" I asked lamely. I turned to face him. It had been weeks since I'd seen him, and he seemed older and more serious somehow. And he was alone.

He laughed. "Because you forget your

gloves every Christmas Eve. I think you've got a secret desire to get frostbite and stay home from school the whole winter."

"No, that's not it at all," I protested.

"There's only one remedy for cold hands, you know," he said patiently. Before I could object, he lifted my hands out of my pockets and began rubbing my fingers gently, one by one. His hands were incredibly warm on mine, and I felt my fingers start to tingle almost immediately.

"They're really fine," I said stiffly, wondering what in the world this was all leading to. Did he really think I'd get frostbite, or was it something more?

"Well, I think you've got the circulation back now," he said, dropping my hands unexpectedly. That certainly answered my question! I thought, stuffing them quickly back in my pockets. He stood looking at me for a long moment, his expression unreadable. "We're next," he said softly.

"What?" I answered blankly.

He smiled, very much in control of the situation. "We're next for the cider," he said patiently, and I could feel myself flushing.

"Oh, the cider," I blurted out, and he grinned.

"You were a million miles away," he offered as we stepped up to the counter.

No, just four thousand. The distance between New York and Rome. He gingerly handed me a cup of steaming cider, and guided me away from the crowd. "Want to grab a seat over there?" He pointed to a wrought-iron bench a few feet away. "Or are you with someone tonight?"

"No, I'm alone." I looked directly into his eyes, and thought of the pale blue letter lying on the kitchen table. "Carlo's gone back to Italy."

"I know," he said, and his tone was gentle.

"Sherry?" I said questioningly.

"She's with her parents tonight," he said, taking a careful sip of the cider as we sat down. We were silent for a moment, watching the musicians take their places on the bandstand for the traditional Christmas concert.

I studied Andy's face, the strong, even features half shadowed under the muted glow of a streetlight. He looked the same, and yet different. A friend, and a stranger. So much had happened to me in the past few months, that it had never occurred to me that Andy would change, too. But he had. There was a strength in his face that I hadn't seen before, and when he turned his warm brown eyes to me, they seemed filled with hidden secrets.

"It's good to see you," he said simply. "I've missed you."

I tried to smile, but my mouth felt dry, and I couldn't force any words past my lips. I've missed you, *cara*.

Carlo's words. Andy's face.

He was waiting for me to say something. "It wouldn't seem like Christmas Eve without you," I said clumsily.

He put down the cider and his hand closed over mine. "Another Christmas Eve together. Can't break with tradition, can we?" He smiled.

"No, of course not." I smiled back.

The flutist stepped to the podium then, and a strong, sweet sound filled the night air. "Silent Night." It was hauntingly beautiful, and I could feel a lump form in my throat. I quickly ran my hand over my eyes to brush away the tears that lurked there, but Andy was too quick for me.

"Don't cry tonight, Jamie," he said softly, and he gently wiped away my tears. "There's too much to look forward to."

He gave my hand a little squeeze then and turned his attention back to the bandstand. The band had picked up the tempo with some bright Christmas songs, and one of the musicians was jangling a set of silver sleigh bells in time to "Jingle Bells."

I stared at Andy, trying to sort out my

feelings. There's too much to look forward to, he had said. Did he mean for each of us separately, or together?

I thought of Carlo, thousands of miles away, enjoying himself at a party, or at home with his family, alive, vital, with those dark eyes and that irrepressible grin. There would never be anyone like Carlo. Never.

Would our paths cross again? I wanted to believe that they would. Too much had happened in the past few months for me to ever forget him.

And Andy? What lay ahead for the two of us?

"Andy," I started, just as the rollicking strains of "Jingle Bells" faded.

"Shhh," he said, putting his finger on my lips. He pointed to the bell tower, just as the chimes pierced the cold night air. Twelve chimes.

"It's midnight," he said, looking deeply into my eyes. "Merry Christmas, Jamie." His look was tender, his voice was feather-soft, and it was impossible to tell just what he was trying to say.

I took a deep breath and decided to put all my questions aside and enjoy the magic of the moment. The glittering tree, the razor-sharp wind, the bittersweet sound of the bells — all would be etched on my memory forever. And Andy, too.

Impulsively, I kissed Andy's cheek, caught up in the wonder of the night.

"Merry Christmas, Andy," I echoed.

I smiled at him, and I felt a warm glow rush through me. It came from a deep well-spring within me, and I recognized it immediately. It was a feeling both familiar and precious.

It was Christmas, and I was happy. And what would happen to me and Carlo, and me and Andy, who could tell?